Lily... Laura

Carol Di Prima

PAGE PUBLISHING, INC.
Conneaut Lake, PA

First originally published by Page Publishing 2020

ISBN 978-1-6624-1137-3 (pbk)
ISBN 978-1-6624-1138-0 (digital)

Printed in the United States of America

Chapter 1

Laura told her friends that she would not be walking home from school with them today. She lied to Luca and I. C., her two best friends, that she had to run an errand for her mom. It was one month to the day her seven-year-old brother, Andy, disappeared. She didn't want to go home. She couldn't bear to listen to her mom whimpering in her bedroom when she thought that her cries were unheard. She no longer wanted to see the pain in her older brother's eyes as he tried to hide it by spending more time in his room or with his friends.

I'm the one who's responsible, a voice inside her cried out.

Laura wanted to disappear; she didn't want to think or feel. The guilt had become insufferable for the twelve-year-old. She didn't want to be Laura Stephens, the seventh-grade student at Parker Middle School. She wanted to erase that horrible night that changed her life as she knew it. She desperately wanted things to go back to the way they were. If only she were able to go back in time and change the events of that dreadful night. *But that only happens in science-fiction movies, video games, or fantasy books,* Laura sadly thought.

As Laura walked away from her friends, Luca called out to her.

"There's something you should know, Laura," he whispered.

"What is it?" Laura sensed that she was not going to like what he had to say.

Luca lowered his head and avoided eye contact. "Well, this morning we overheard some girls whispering, and they mentioned your name and…" Luca stammered. "And they were saying that…" Luca couldn't continue.

"There's a malicious rumor circulating in the school that your father is a coward and that he did nothing to help Andy," interjected I. C. "They said that your father may have something to do with it and is considered a suspect," I. C. continued. It took a few seconds for Laura to comprehend and make sense of what the boys said. Her eyes welled up. She gazed at Luca and then at I. C. in disbelief. The hurt that she had been feeling paled to the anger she felt now. Her hands made fists as her fingernails dug into the palms of her hands.

"We thought we should tell you before you find out from someone else," I. C. said apologetically. "Sorry, Laura."

"These girls—do you know them?" Laura swallowed hard as she waited for the answer.

"I don't. You probably don't either. And besides, I distinctly remember one of them saying that she had heard it from someone else and that that girl had heard it from someone else, etcetera, etcetera…"

"She gets the idea that we don't know who started it, I. C." Luca was annoyed.

Laura clenched her teeth. "How can someone be so mean to say something like that about my father?"

"It certainly can't be any of your friends."

"A friend wouldn't say that about your father," Luca added.

The boys didn't know how to comfort Laura, their friend since second grade.

Luca quickly changed the subject and asked, "Do you want us to come with you?" Laura did not answer and looked puzzled. "You said your mom wants you to do something. You want us to come?"

"What? Oh…no. Thanks, guys. I'm gonna go now."

"Do you have an umbrella? The forecast called for rain, and it might change to ice if the temperature drops," I. C. added.

"I'll be okay," Laura answered. She tried to sound calm, but the rage inside her would have set an iceberg into flames. She'd burst if she didn't find an outlet.

Laura continued to walk aimlessly away from her middle school. She had not thought about where she'd go; she just wanted to keep moving.

The air was getting damp and heavy. Her steps took on a faster pace as the tragic night surfaced in her thoughts. The same scenes kept playing over and over as if it were a video with a defective replay button. She recalled how anxious she had been as she waited for her father to return from the local pharmacy with the brown bobby pins that she had wanted. That night was to be very special; she was going to make her dancing debut, and everything had to be perfect. Her mother had pointed out to Laura that she had black bobby pins and that the trip to the store was needless. Laura, however, insisted on having brown ones so that they would be a better match for her blond hair. Laura's father realized that she was having a bad case of nerves and agreed to run the errand. He didn't want to add to her anxiety—not now. As he got his jacket and car keys, Andy begged to go with him and trailed behind. Mr. Stephens held his son's hand and walked out of the house into the cold December night and drove off to get brown bobby pins for his daughter.

As Laura's mother helped her with the makeup, Laura rehearsed the dancing steps as she envisioned her role as a Spanish dancer in *The Nutcracker* ballet. In less than an hour, she was to report to the backstage of the auditorium of Parker Middle School. Although she had performed in *The Nutcracker* many times through the years, this role was unlike the others. Those roles required little or no choreography. Laura's heart had ached to dance; she yearned for an important role, a meatier role. She wanted to give a performance that required coordination and grace—one that demanded her steps to be precise like the rhythmic beat of a perfect heart. She wanted a part that required her to wear a colorful classic tutu. The word *tutu* always brought a smile to her face. The sound of it made her giggle.

She recalled the moment when her ballet teacher had given her the thrilling news that she had landed the dancing part after several auditions. She was finally going to dance in the annual holiday performance of *The Nutcracker*.

Laura remembered staring at the tutu that she was to wear as one of the Spanish dancers. She blushed as she recalled looking at the red ruffles and the black top with a slightly lower V-neck than her mom would have allowed her to wear. Laura sadly recalled the blaring sirens that had ended her mental rehearsal. Such wailing sounds were not heard very often in the quiet suburb that boasted to be less than a forty-minute ride on the Metro-North Railroad to New York City. The shrill of the sirens had unsettled her as if it had been an omen that something horrible was about to change her life. She remembered the conversation that was etched in her memory.

"What's taking Daddy so long, Mom? We have to leave soon."

"There's plenty of time, Laura. They'll be here. Andy probably wants something from the toy section and your father is thinking of ways to talk him out of it," Mrs. Stephens cheerfully responded. She recounted a funny story about Andy to distract her daughter and soothe her nerves. As she was about to end it, she abruptly left Laura's side to answer the phone that begged to be picked up.

"Yes, this is she. WHAT HAPPENED? I'M ON MY WAY!" she screamed.

"Laura, there's been an accident. Daddy is at the hospital. Get your jacket." Mrs. Stephen's cries and the alarming look on her face instantly erased Laura's dancing debut from her thoughts.

When they had arrived at the hospital, her father was being treated for bruises, lacerations, and a broken arm in the emergency room. Laura could not forget the look on his face as he lay in the hospital bed.

"Jonathan, are you all right? How's Andy? Where is he?" Mrs. Stephens asked without taking a breath.

"I'm fine, Elaine. I'm fine. I don't know," he answered. They both turned to the nurse.

"You were brought in alone," the nurse answered.

"No, no…my son was in the car with me. My son, Andy, was in the car with me," he repeated, as his voice grew louder and louder.

"I'll go check the other rooms," she answered and walked out.

"Dad," Laura called out, "what happened? You're bleeding."

"Jonathan, do you remember what happened?" Neither Laura's mother nor Laura got an answer. Mr. Stephens stared at his daughter and his wife as if he had heard those questions for the first time. Laura cried as she hugged her mom. "I think he's in shock, Laura."

Andy went missing that night and had not been seen since.

"Look where you're going! Wait for the green light." A harsh voice snapped Laura out of her trance. Realizing that she was crossing the street on a red light, she dashed back to the sidewalk. She felt the cold wind on her face as the cars zoomed by. She tried to settle her mind and keep calm, but the sudden burst of rain upset her. I. C. had warned her about the rainstorm. She should have listened to him. Although everyone called him a geek and complained about his nerdy ways, he was touted as being one of the smartest kids in the school; he was annoyingly right about mostly everything. Many ridiculed him, including his best friend Luca, and that sometimes caused arguments and bickering between the boys.

Laura thought about the rumor and her brother's disappearance and cried. The pain became insurmountable, and her anxiety escalated. She needed to do something; she needed something to focus on. Questions flooded her mind: *Who took Andy? Where could he be? Who started the rumor? How can I stop it?* Although she couldn't answer the questions about her brother, she was determined to find the culprit who started the rumors about her father.

She wanted to continue walking and keep moving to clear her head, but there was a turn in the weather. Ice pellets were falling on her head and the ground. She decided to head back home and hastened her pace. She lowered her head and kept her eyes on the slippery ground. As she walked, she had an eerie feeling that someone was watching her. She turned around several times, but she didn't notice anyone who aroused suspicion. Everyone was scurrying to get indoors or opening umbrellas. Laura put her book bag over her head and walked faster. She took several steps, and suddenly everything went black.

For an instant, she opened her eyes and saw a crowd of people hovering above her. They spoke among themselves, but their words were muffled, indiscernible. She thought she heard someone say "Call 911" and "She just collapsed." The faces became blurry and then faded away; all went black again as if someone had suddenly flicked the lights. In the darkness, she had the strange sensation that she was being swooped up into the sky and was floating up, away from the crowd, from everything.

Laura awoke and was bowled over by what she saw. *How did I get home?* She had not mouthed the words, yet an elderly woman pulled up a chair next to Laura's bed and answered her. "You're safe, Laura, and we're in a…well, I guess you can call it your room inside a giant bubble, but from where I come from, we call it a ccass'a, but there's no need for you to remember that," she chuckled.

Laura looked at her surroundings. She *was* in her room lying in *her* bed. Everything looked exactly the same except for the walls and the floor; they were transparent.

"This is so weird," Laura called out. As she left the bed to touch the walls, the bed folded itself up and vanished. "Wow, did you see that?" Laura cried out.

"Yes, that's how things operate here. I wanted you to feel safe, so the bubble became a duplicate of your room, a place that is familiar to you."

She looked through the curved wall of the bubble, and to her astonishment, it was suspended in air. She looked up and saw clouds that looked like a cotton candy machine had spun out of control; they were huge. The purple, red, and blue puffy clouds appeared sticky as if they had been sugarcoated and were ready to be eaten. She looked down at the transparent floor and saw the place where she had fainted. Strange—she was able to see it from that height. She remembered what had happened to her but didn't understand why she had collapsed. She felt fine now—vibrant. She felt more alive than she had been for a long while. *Why am I here? Who is she?*

"Laura," the elderly woman began, "I've been watching you and had to come in unexpectedly because you need me. I had hoped that you wouldn't need me so soon, but today's incident was a warning. It's the first sign that you are in terrible danger. We don't have much time here in the ccass'a, the bubble." The elderly woman's tone took a turn.

"I'm in danger? You mean like my brother? Where's Andy?" Laura cried out.

"I come from another dimension and have been summoned to help you, but whether or not you survive depends on the actions you take from this day forth. It's up to you, Laura. We have to go now."

Before Laura could utter another iota, every piece of furniture and the contents of the room folded up neatly into squares, rectangles, triangles, and shapes that defied geometric classification. Everything before her vanished.

Soon after, Laura found herself in front of her house without any memory of her encounter with the woman or the incident in the rain. Her heavy winter jacket, black jeans, and black sneakers were drenched. She hurried inside wishing she had taken the umbrella that stood in front of her in the umbrella stand. She removed her sneakers and dashed to the kitchen to grab something to eat.

Chapter 2

T he rumors about Laura's father did not end; they spun out of control. Laura was determined to find the source, but misguided accusations distanced many of her girlfriends. Laura's life became enveloped in unanswered questions. Her thoughts were everywhere except where they should have been. The only thread that she was able to hold on to was I. C. and Luca's friendship, but even that relationship became shaky. Laura's hurtful remarks strained their relationship when she alluded that maybe she should add them to her list of suspects. She had said it on impulse, without thinking. Despite the accusations, I. C.'s heroic efforts helped Laura get passing grades in all her courses except math. She was warned that if her class work and test scores didn't improve, she would fail the course. The thought sickened her; she had never failed a test, let alone an entire course.

Luca and I. C. made valiant attempts to maintain their friendship with Laura. Each day, they continued to walk home together as if nothing had happened. Soon after Laura had accused them, I. C. and Luca talked about it. I. C. led the conversation as he explained to Luca that Laura needed them now more than ever if she were to get over this crisis. He further explained that Laura had become obsessed with finding the person responsible for the rumors. Luca listened to I. C. as he described the behavior to be expected.

"He must be hitting the psychology books," Luca muttered to himself and tried not to seem bored. He knew that I. C. wanted to help Laura as much as he did. They both longed for their old Laura to return.

I. C. initiated conversations on their way home each day from school hoping that Laura would not just respond with the usual short answers or shrugging of the shoulders. Surprisingly, she showed interest today. Laura's deep-green eyes moved from face to face as they spoke. She even smiled once or twice, to the delight of her friends who had missed her immensely. Laura was about to say something to I. C. but instead ran toward an elderly woman with a brown cane who was stepping into the street.

"Oh no! You're going to get hit by that car!" She grabbed the woman's arm and pulled her back to the curb. I. C. ran to catch up to Laura, but he fell. As he landed on the floor, his cell phone fell out of his back pocket. He quickly examined it and put it back in his pocket.

"I'm sorry if I pulled you too hard," Laura said. "But you kept walking, and that car was coming...you okay?" she asked her.

"Yes," the woman answered. "Thank you, child." She was frightened and looked disoriented. I. C. and Luca joined the elderly woman with the brown cane.

"The light was red. Didn't you see it?" Laura asked.

"My eyes are failing me," the woman answered as they all crossed the street safely. The woman went directly to the green bench that faced Centennial Bank. She slowly sat down and put her rubber-bottomed cane close to her side.

"Are you blind?" asked Luca.

"Partially," she answered.

"Is your blindness caused by a disease? What's the name of your disease?" I. C. asked. He instinctively pulled his cell phone out of his pocket, ready to locate and define the woman's illness.

"Put that away and stop your mumbo jumbo," complained Luca. Laura witnessed the familiar scene between I. C. and Luca. She glanced at I. C. who sulked as he looked down at his electronic gadget. Laura then stared at Luca with her catlike eyes. She had had enough! When was Luca going to stop complaining about I. C.? And when was I. C. going to stop acting like a nerd?

"When are you two going to stop arguing?" I. C. put his cell phone away and looked at the woman.

"I'm usually safe when I go out," the woman began. "I don't know what happened today. I should have been more careful. I want to thank all of you, especially you—what's your name, child?"

"I'm Laura. This is Luca, and that's—"

"Let me introduce myself," interjected I. C. "I'm I. C."

"Icy. That's a very unusual name," the woman said.

"Yes, it is," I. C. replied. "It's not a conventional name. It's just two letters." Luca was about to say something, but Laura elbowed him.

"It's capital *I*, period, capital *C*, period," he explained.

"Oh, I see!" exclaimed the woman. I. C. broke into a roar of laughter.

"Don't you get it?" he asked. No one answered.

"I. C., Icy, and then she said, 'I see,'" he explained, still laughing.

"Can we go now?" asked Luca, sounding annoyed.

"Go, children. I'm fine now. Thank you again."

The boys began walking away, and Laura trailed behind them. She turned around to glance at the elderly woman. She had a strange feeling that they had met before. She stopped walking and watched as the elderly woman took a deep breath and slowly patted her hair down on her head with both hands. She started at the tip of her forehead as she felt the hair in its proper place. Each movement of the fingers led her to the back of her neck, to her grayish-white bun. The wrinkles around her brown eyes were many, for she was a woman in her seventies. The lines of time, however, did not take away the angelic look that graced her face.

"Laura, are you coming?" Luca interrupted Laura's daze. "It's getting late!" he screamed from a half-block away.

"I'm right behind you," she answered.

Laura turned around once more to look at the woman, and for an instant, she thought her eyes were playing tricks on her. The old woman was surrounded by a bright white light that was going on and off like a light switch. She rubbed her eyes and quickly opened them to take another look, but she was gone. Luca's voice redirected her attention to the boys.

"Are we friends?" Luca asked her.

"I wanna be sure that you had nothing to do with those rumors about my father."

"I swear, Laura, I never said a word, and neither did I. C.," answered Luca, pointing to I. C.

"I can't believe that you would even think that. We've been friends since second grade, and you suspect us?" I. C. asked.

Laura glanced at Luca and then turned to I. C. "Sorry, guys. I am so upset...I can hardly think straight...and Andy...we'll never see Andy again...We need a miracle. That's what we need." She sobbed. Luca and I. C. became teary-eyed as their friend continued to cry. They didn't know what to say or do.

"I'm gonna find out who started it, and when I do..." Laura wiped her tears.

"He or she will have to answer to me!" I. C. interjected.

"And me!" echoed Luca. The three of them continued walking at a faster pace. Laura's thoughts drifted back to the old woman. The feeling that they had met nagged her.

Chapter 3

L aura paced back and forth in her room. It was Sunday night, and she knew that she would have to give the bad news to her mom sooner or later. The test paper had to be signed and handed in. She stared at the math test score until her eyes burned. The letter *F* was written at the top of the paper near her name. She had shown the test paper only to I. C. a few days ago. She had lamented that she was a failure in math and a failure in finding the culprit. She was a failure, period. She felt uncomfortable in school and thought of cutting classes, but that idea soon left her. I. C. quickly discounted it as being ludicrous. She recalled him saying, "It will be counterproductive." He also warned Laura that he would not help her with her math if she went through with her plan. He repeatedly told her that the rumor would go away in time and that the best thing she could do was to ignore it. She missed Andy, and the thought of him added to her guilt.

With paper in hand, she walked out of her room to have her mom sign it. She nervously bit her lip and walked toward the master bedroom. On the way, she passed by her brother Jeff's room. He would probably know how to give the bad news to Mom.

She was about to walk in but stopped when she heard voices. Jeff was whispering to his girlfriend, Ronnie. She took advantage of the house rule that the bedroom door had to be left ajar when she or her brother had friends in their rooms. She peeked and saw them kissing. She giggled as she watched them and quietly went downstairs unnoticed. She would think of a way to give the news to her mom while she ate her favorite snack, a piece of baklava, a Greek pastry made with phyllo dough filled with honey and chopped walnuts. A class trip to a Greek restaurant had introduced her to the new snack. She drank a glass of grapefruit juice with it—her wacky idea to reduce the sweetness of the honey. Her mom made sure that baklava was part of her grocery list and bought a batch of it at the gourmet shop close to her real estate office once a week. Laura held the test paper in one hand as the other reached for the grapefruit juice and poured a glass. She then searched for the baklava; she moved jars and bottles around on the shelves, but she couldn't find any.

She always brings them home on Sundays. I can't drink this without the baklava.

Annoyed, Laura left the kitchen and went back upstairs to her mom's bedroom, near her room. She took a deep breath and was about to knock, but her hand froze in midair. Laura heard her mom whimpering. She quickly turned around and went to her room instead. She closed the door behind her, tore the test paper, and threw herself on her bed. She put both arms over her eyes and lay still. Her mother was crying, and she knew why; it was because of her selfishness. If she had settled for the black bobby pins, her father would not have gone to the pharmacy and the accident would never have happened and Andy would not be missing. Her mother told her many times that she shouldn't feel guilty. She reminded Laura that the police had not stopped their search and that they should not lose hope that Andy would be found. She also begged Laura to see a counselor, but Laura refused to go. She was not a mental case.

As she wept, the anger became even more directed toward herself. The video that had stopped playing in her mind for a short while played again. She tried to stop it. She tried to pause it, but it wouldn't. Her emotions tired her; her damp eyes felt heavy. She fought to keep them open, but she allowed them to rest and drifted into a deep sleep. She soon woke up and looked at her alarm clock. The white digital numbers showed 7:23. What had seemed like a long nap only lasted for twenty minutes, and she knew that she had dreamed.

That was a weird dream.

She couldn't get a grasp of the flashing images of the strange dream. The images didn't make sense. Someone was giving her a warning. About what? Andy's face was fading in and out, and then she saw him marching like a soldier. She couldn't shake the unsettling feeling. "Andy," she called out repeatedly. She looked around her room searching for her brother, and finally she muttered, "Just a dream. It was only a dream." Laura left the bed and stood up in front of the long mirror. She recalled the day her father hung it on the wall. She and Andy had watched him as he measured the wall and the mirror several times so that it would be precisely in the middle of the wall between her closet and the window. Laura had just turned seven when her mom brought little Andy home from the hospital. At first, she resented him. He had no business being part of *her* family. She begged her mother to return him to the hospital several times. She remembered being jealous of him. She couldn't understand why everyone made such a fuss over him. After all, he couldn't do anything. She couldn't play with him, nor could she talk to him. He was just there. Laura barely acknowledged her brother's presence. Her attitude toward him changed when he tried to say her name. At first she heard him say "Loa," then it changed to "Lota," and finally it became "Lora." That was when she realized that he was calling her. From that day on, Andy became Laura's baby brother.

Why can't things go back to the way they used to be?

Laura glanced around the room. Each object awoke a memory. The brown teddy bear reminded her of the time her father won it for her at the street bazaar. The porcelain blue-and-white ballet shoes that hung over her bed reminded her of the business trip her father had taken to Washington, DC. Upon his return, he surprised her with the ballet slippers to show how delighted he was that Laura had decided to take ballet lessons. Laura stopped going to ballet school after the accident. And she wasn't going back!

"None of this would've happened if I didn't want to look perfect that night," she called out.

She went back on the bed, lay still, and stared at the ceiling. She envisioned her family without her. *Without me, the family would be perfect,* she thought. *Everyone would be better off without me.*

She decided that she'd leave home in the morning. She packed a few things in her backpack and went to bed. First, she lay on her back, and then she turned to her favorite side—her left—and lay still waiting to fall asleep. She brushed away strands of hair from her eyes and turned again to her original position. She slowly fell asleep and had the same dream she had earlier. Laura's body suddenly jerked. She sat up, and with eyes wide open, she saw the face of the elderly woman she had pulled back to the curb on her way home from school with the boys. Her face had a bright glow. Laura smiled at her and closed her eyes. She lay back, turned on her favorite side, and went back to sleep.

It was Monday morning; Laura followed the same routine she had followed since she was a sixth-grader at Parker Middle School. After breakfast, she normally walked to school; but this morning, she had a different plan. She looked inside her backpack and wondered if she needed anything. Yes—she needed money. She only had the lunch money her mom had given her for the week. She climbed on her bed and took down the porcelain ballet shoes. On the back of each shoe, she had taped two neatly folded ten-dollar bills. She removed the bills carefully so as not to rip them. She then went to the teddy bear and unzipped the back. She put her fingers inside the foam that shaped it and extracted all the dollar bills that she had hidden in it. Out came the bills, all fifteen of them. This was her "emergency fund," as I. C. called it. Everybody should have one. She had three five-dollar bills, one ten-dollar bill, and eleven one-dollar bills. She thought she had more than that. Her fingers kept searching and feeling their way inside the foam, but nothing. She became flustered and saw the numbers on the digital clock change. It was getting late. She threw the shoes and the bear on her bed and quietly closed the door. She paused and again asked herself what else did she need? A cell phone. She needed a cell phone but didn't have one. She passed Jeff's room and listened for sounds but didn't hear any. He was in the shower. She slowly opened his door and looked for his cell phone. Laura did something that she had never done before in her entire life. She took something that did not belong to her. She knew it was wrong but felt she had to do it. She put the cell phone in her backpack and shoved all the neatly folded bills on the side and closed the zipper. She walked downstairs to the kitchen and took one last look before she left.

Laura's life was taking a dramatic turn for the worse.

Chapter 4

L aura walked past her middle school and walked four blocks west toward the Metro-North Railroad Station. The bitter cold nipped her neck as the wind blew at her scarf. Her feet were getting cold too, and she looked forward to boarding the warm train. She tucked her hair inside her jacket, raised the collar, and tied the scarf around it. Her steps hastened to escape the frigid air.

She had come to this station many times with her parents to take the Hudson Metro-North to Manhattan when her father didn't want to deal with the snail-paced traffic or when he wanted to avoid driving endlessly around the city blocks for a parking space. They usually went during the holiday season, when the city overflowed with the sights, sounds, and aromas of the festive season. They had feasted their eyes numerous times on the huge celebratory Christmas tree dressed with thousands of multicolored lights at Rockefeller Center. The smell of hot pretzels and roasted chestnuts enveloped them as they watched the ice-skaters dance to the holiday tunes. Afterward, they'd walk or take a bus to admire the holiday window displays at Bergdorf Goodman, Bloomingdale's, Lord & Taylor, or Macy's. One year, they went to a tree-lighting ceremony in Dante Park at the Upper West Side Lincoln Square area. The whole neighborhood was transformed into a winter wonderland with street performers, music, lots of food, and fun activities for children. But the trip that was foremost in her mind was the time her family went to see *The Nutcracker* ballet at the New York State Theater in Lincoln Center. This was her introduction to the world of ballet.

"They're dancing on their toes!" she had exclaimed to her mom. "Isn't that painful...and hard?" Her mom had responded that it was both painful and hard and required a lot of dedication and practice. From that day forward, she decided that she wanted to take ballet lessons and that perhaps one day she'd be good enough to dance on her toes on a stage. Her last memory made her weep. The opening night performance, the bobby pins, and the accident all surfaced again. She made a conscious effort to stop it. She was not going to think about it. She scolded herself for doing it and was going to pinch herself every time those thoughts came to her. She bought a ticket and sat down by a woman who was fast asleep with a newspaper on her lap. That suited her just fine. She didn't want to talk to anyone and possibly have to carry on a conversation. She was determined not to think about anything unpleasant. She looked at the commuters around her and tried to guess what type of work they did. Yes, that was what she'd do. She forced herself to play the mental game, but it was hard to concentrate. It was like swallowing a teaspoon of awful-tasting medicine. She then thought that perhaps she should try to take a nap. She closed her eyes, took deep breaths, and thought of nothing. She had to pinch herself several times, as that tactic didn't work either. She stopped fighting with herself and waited for the train to reach her stop.

Laura exited the train along with its passengers at Grand Central Station. More memories flooded her mind, but she stopped them from taking over; she didn't want to remember. She walked until she found an exit that led her to the street. The burst of cold air was refreshing, but soon she felt the coldness in her bones. She zipped up her winter jacket and tied the scarf around her neck again. The sidewalks bustled with people getting to work. Many carried a briefcase in one hand and a steaming hot cup of coffee in the other. Some carried their bag on their shoulders, and still others—mainly women—carried a shoulder bag, a briefcase, and a cup of coffee. They all seemed to be in a hurry and were focused on reaching their workplace. Laura lost herself in her new setting. The towering buildings, the elegant shops, the theaters with colorful marquees, the bill-boards with famous faces, and the busy streets of Manhattan made her feel as if she had no identity or history. She had no past to contemplate, no present to worry about, and no future to ponder. The feeling of nothingness soothed her.

She thought of getting something hot to drink and warm up a bit. She needed to find a coffee shop that might serve her a hot cup of cocoa. She wondered where she was and looked up at the sign. Park Avenue. She didn't remember ever walking there, but she thought finding a coffee shop shouldn't be too difficult. She kept walking on Park Avenue and spotted a sign that read Midtown Coffee Shop. She walked in and sat at the counter. She quickly ordered a hot cocoa and a blueberry muffin. The waitress, who seemed to have had bad experiences with kids, asked if she had money to pay for the order. Laura reached into her backpack and showed her a ten-dollar bill. The woman gave her a wry smile and quickly served her.

Laura left the coffee shop feeling warmer as she walked down the streets. She gazed at the storefront windows of some elegant shops and went inside a couple of them when she needed to warm up. She felt uncomfortable walking around inside one of them when a saleslady followed her around like a puppy and repeatedly asked if she needed assistance. She sensed that she was suspected of being a juvenile shoplifter. Laura wanted to tell her that she was not going to steal anything and that she just wanted to warm up. She opted instead to leave and not start trouble.

What should she do next? She thought of going to the movies. That would certainly be a great place to keep warm. Her goal now was to find a movie theater. She continued to walk for a long while and noticed that the streets took on a different appearance. There were less shops, restaurants, and buildings and more parking lots, with parking prices plastered on brick walls and metal fences. She became uncomfortable with what she saw and decided to retrace her steps and go back toward the train station. There was a lot more activity there. Her steps seemed to take her still further into less populated streets. She looked up to see where she was. Eleventh Avenue. She knew she had to get back to Park Avenue and Forty-Second

Street. She needed to ask someone to direct her. She saw a small deli and was about to go in when she heard someone say, "Hey, kid, can you help me out?" Laura turned her head and heard a rustling sound underneath a pile of newspapers and large pieces of cardboard. Laura gasped when she saw a man emerge from the mound. He pushed away the cardboard and a layer of newspapers and tried to sit up against the wall. After a short struggle, he steadied himself. A strong disgusting odor of urine emanated from him, similar to that of the girls' bathroom at the end of the school day. His face was dirty, and he was missing two front teeth. His tangled shoulder-length hair and unkempt beard covered most of his dirty face. Despite his bad odor and filthy appearance, Laura did not walk away. As they looked at each other, Laura was taken by his blue-speckled eyes that pleaded for help. Laura had come across homeless individuals on the trips she had taken with her family, but she had never made contact. She was afraid of him, but he looked frail and harmless. She felt sorry for him, and her compassion took over common sense.

"What do you want?"

The man got up on his feet, which were wrapped in newspapers and plastic bags, and put out his hand. "Got some money? I'm hungry." He was wearing layers of grimy T-shirts and an oversize jacket with stains and holes. As he spoke, Laura smelled something else besides urine.

"I'll get you food from the deli. How about a sandwich?"

"Nah…just give me the money, kid. Just give me the money. I'll get my own food. Just give me the money." The persistency in his tone alarmed her.

"I don't have much, and I need it." Her hands trembled as she reached for the backpack. She hesitated and then gave him a few dollars. The homeless man eyed the backpack and grabbed it from her. Laura tried to get it back, but she was no match for him. Laura wouldn't give up. That was her money that she had saved. The thought of losing it and Jeff's cell phone angered her more. She wished that some passerby would help, but there was no one around.

"Hey, give it back. It's mine!" she yelled repeatedly.

The man took several steps back, and his filthy left hand reached for an empty bottle that was hidden under the pile that had sheltered him. He broke the bottle against the wall and held the jagged edges in front of Laura's face. Laura was terrified; she tried to speak, but the words wouldn't come out. She tried to scream, but her vocal cords shut down. She felt like she was in a nightmare where she was being chased by a faceless creature but couldn't scream or call for help. Laura gasped for air but couldn't breathe. She lost consciousness and fell to the ground. The homeless man stared at her and expected her to get up. But Laura did not move, nor was she breathing; her face was turning blue.

"Hey, kid, wake up...wake up. Somebody help—the kid needs help," he hollered. He wobbled to the deli to get help. He turned his head to see if she had moved and was bewildered by what he saw. "What the... What was that—Nah...I'm seeing things." The man looked at the remains of the broken liquor bottle in his hand and threw it away. Laura had vanished. He went back to the pile of newspapers and cardboard and crept under it as if nothing had happened.

Laura woke up inside the bubble that was now familiar. Again, she found herself in her room inside the transparent round fixture surrounded with the cotton candy clouds and the furniture that folded itself up. She stood in front of the elderly woman holding on to her backpack. She didn't recall her name.

"You're safe, Laura, but our time here is very limited."

"I've been here before. I remember. You keep helping me. Why?"

"I cannot control your actions. You have free will. I can only help you when you need me. I appeared to you in your room. Do you remember? I tried to warn you in your dreams because you put yourself in dangerous situations to avoid your pain and guilt. You can't hurry the healing process in this dimension." The woman sighed and looked away. "He knows," she muttered. "I have to keep you safe."

"What did you see?"

"We need to go. Now!" The woman placed her hand on Laura's shoulder, and everything in front of her disappeared.

Chapter 5

L aura was transported back to her warm bed. The trip to the city and her second visit to the bubble were wiped from her memory. The alarm clock went off, but her sleepy eyes didn't want to welcome the day. As she stretched and yawned, her feet felt something heavy weighing on them. She sat up and saw her porcelain ballet slippers, the brown teddy bear, and her backpack at the foot of the bed. "How did they get here?" she muttered to herself. She checked to see if her emergency fund was where it should be and was relieved to see that it was. She grabbed the teddy bear, the porcelain slippers, and the backpack and returned them to their proper places.

She got that eerie feeling again. It gnawed at her like a mouse gnawing on a piece of cheese. She couldn't quite put her finger on it. The feeling was similar to the one she had last night. She continued her normal morning routine and got ready for school.

On her way to school, she heard the sound of a familiar ringtone. As it kept ringing, she realized it was Jeff's, but where was it coming from? She asked herself, "Where is it? It's coming from my backpack?" She asked out loud, "How did you get in there?" Laura asked the phone as if she expected it to respond. She looked at the phone and saw "Ronnie." Laura was flustered and very confused. She wanted to answer it but decided against it. How would she explain having Jeff's phone to Ronnie? Laura was very troubled but couldn't address that now. She had to get to school. She turned it off and made a mental note to return it to his room as soon as she got home from school.

That afternoon, Laura ran upstairs to Jeff's room to return his phone, but he was there. She froze when she saw him. He was turning his room upside down searching for his cell phone. Laura had no choice but to tell him where it was. She explained to him that she found the phone in her backpack and didn't know how it got there.

"You don't know how it got there? Were you walking in your sleep when you stole it from me?" Somehow that triggered a memory. It was vague, but as she stared at the phone, broken images of how it got inside her backpack startled her.

"Are you gonna answer? Did you steal my phone?"

Laura was distraught by the images. She then remembered discovering the ballet slippers and the teddy bear on her bed, and she had no recollection of how they had gotten there either. Nothing made sense. Was she losing her mind? Her blank look and long silence infuriated Jeff. He wanted answers.

"I don't know, Jeff. I don't know," she finally said.

"How dare you steal my phone? I'm telling Mom tonight."

Mrs. Stephens sighed when Jeff gave her the news that night. She climbed up the six steps leading to the bedrooms. Each step up was like a hurdle to her. With bent shoulders, she held on to the wooden banister that led her to the top of the stairs. She stopped in front of Laura's door and took several short breaths before she knocked.

"Laura, can I come in?" Laura opened the door and went back to her desk. Mrs. Stephens sat at the edge of Laura's bed. As she glanced at her reflection in the mirror, she put her fingers through her hair and pushed it away from her face. She was surprised to see that her temples were turning gray. She looked old, much older than her forty-five years. The accident and Andy's disappearance had taken a toll on her. She missed her youngest son and the husband whom she knew that had been taken away from her. She stood up and straightened her shoulders in defiance.

"Jeff said that you've been mean to him and that you took his phone. Did you take it?" Mrs. Stephens didn't get a response. "Laura, have you been listening to what I've said? I asked you a question."

"Yeah, Mom."

"Well, did you take it?"

"No, Mom. I mean…yeah, I did…I really don't know for sure."

Mrs. Stephens was exasperated. "You're not sure? I've mentioned this before, but this time I'm going to insist. We, all of us, as a family will go to a counselor. I know that you are against it, but—"

"Just because I'm not sure I took the phone?"

"No. You know why we should go." Mrs. Stephens sighed. "We need to talk to a therapist as a family, and when Daddy comes home, he'll join us."

"Daddy left us," Laura blurted out. "He won't be home for a long time."

"You know that's not true. We've discussed this. He'll be home sooner than you think." Mrs. Stephens sighed again, and after a short silence, she began speaking again in a loud whisper. Her tone changed. "If you agree to go to counseling…I'll…replace your cell phone. Please, Laura, this is very important to me, to your brother… to all of us." Mrs. Stephens continued to talk, unaware that Laura was barely listening to her.

"We all have to do this as a family," Mrs. Stephens reiterated. "It will help all of us cope and heal. I'll get you another cell—"

"I don't need a cell phone. What I need is Andy. I want my brother back. That's what I need." Laura's voice cracked. "If I hadn't been so selfish about the bobby pins, Daddy…and…and…Andy would be here."

"This was not your fault, Laura. No one is to blame. We have to be patient. It takes time for the pain to go away. It takes time. We need to believe…and…not give up hope that Andy will return to us." Mrs. Stephens struggled to hold back her tears. Laura sobbed as her mother held her tightly to her chest. She wished that she could take her daughter's pain away. She wished that the accident had never happened; she wished for many things.

Chapter 6

"We've got to do something, guys," Laura said as she and the boys were walking home from school the next day. "Everyone looks at me like I have a disease...or...something worse. Lisa and Jill are avoiding me. We always ate lunch together on Tuesdays, Wednesdays, and Fridays. I ate lunch by myself today again," Laura said, lowering her eyes.

"But today is..." Luca didn't finish his sentence.

"Today is Tuesday," Laura interrupted Luca.

"Good try!" exclaimed I. C. as he patted Luca on the back.

"Even some girls whom I barely know look at me funny and whisper when they see me in the halls," Laura continued to complain.

"What do you want to do?" Luca asked.

"You know what I want to do. I want to find out who started this."

"A rumor is a story passed from one person to another without any known authority for the truth of it, a mere report. Treat it as such. I guarantee you that no one will give it any thought as soon as another piece of gossip grabs everyone's attention," I. C. remarked, sounding like his nerdy self.

"So I'm just supposed to listen to it and do nothing? No, I just can't do nothing anymore! I've got to find the person who started it and have the creep take it back." Laura made her announcement and walked away.

"That's Laura, very independent and—"

27

"And you sound like your nerdy self again," Luca interrupted.

"Jeff once told me that she was like that as a child too," I. C. continued, ignoring Luca's comment. "When she was four years old, her mother took her and Jeff to the movies to see *Sleeping Beauty*. When they got there, she made a loud commotion because she didn't want any help getting out of the car. Even though the door was too heavy for her to open, she insisted on doing it herself. She screamed and attracted so much attention that some people went over to see what was going on. And because of her, they missed the matinee show and had to pay regular prices for the next show."

Luca kept watching Laura walk in front of them as I. C. continued rambling about Laura. He ran up to her, leaving a short distance between them.

"How are you going to find out who started the rumor?" Luca asked, not moving from his spot.

"I don't know. I don't know!" she screamed as she continued to walk faster. Luca looked back and met I. C.'s eyes. He stared at him and then shrugged his shoulders.

"Where is she going?" I. C. asked.

Luca shrugged his shoulders again. "How should I know? Look, she stopped walking." Luca pointed to her.

"She stopped walking because she's at the bus stop. You don't think that she's taking the bus, do you?" I. C.'s eyes bulged.

"I better go to her before she does something stupid," Luca answered.

"Yes, you do that. I'm going to investigate this matter further. I mean…that I'll see what I can find out." I. C. cleared his throat.

"When are you ever going to talk normal?" Luca asked. "You really get on my nerves. Nobody talks like you. Just because you're super smart doesn't mean you have to sound like a super nerd, does it?"

"I can speak like you if I want to. And I don't sound like a nerd," I. C. defended himself and suddenly pointed at Laura. "She's taking the bus! Go stop her!"

Luca ran to the bus, but Laura was already inside looking for a seat.

"Laura, where are you going? Get out of the bus!"

"Young man, are you getting on? If you're not, let go of the door," Luca heard the driver say to him.

"Uh, yeah, I'm getting on. Give me a minute to get the money." Luca put his hands in his pockets and paid the fare. He walked to Laura and sat on the empty seat next to her. "Where are you going?"

"I need to think, and I really don't need you to help me do that. And I don't know where I'm going. I just feel like I have to do something. Where's I. C.?"

"He stayed behind. He's going to 'investigate the matter further,'" Luca mimicked I. C.

"Yeah, right, he's going to investigate," Laura murmured and shook her head.

"You're really letting this rumor thing bother you too much, you know?" Luca whispered.

"You think so? I found a note in my science book this morning." Laura's voice quivered.

"What did it say?"

"It said..." Laura covered her mouth and mumbled, "Your father is a coward. He's responsible for Andy's kidnapping. He belongs in jail, where he is."

"Don't pay attention to that! Whoever wrote it probably wasn't ever your friend to begin with. Just ignore it." Luca paused and then asked, "Did you try to see if you could recognize the handwriting?"

"I couldn't. It was written on the computer and printed out."

"Let it go, Laura. Ignore it."

"I can't ignore it, Luca." Laura suddenly became teary-eyed and looked out the window. "My brother is missing, and my father is gone, and who knows where *he* is," Laura cried.

"Just ignore it, Laura. Ignore it," he repeated. "Let's get out at the next stop and go home."

"It's my father they're talking about, my father...not you...or your family... Now everybody is saying that he's in jail for causing the accident. Just let me think."

"But your mother told you that he's not in jail. You know he's not."

"They're all saying that he is. What if she's...she's...lying to protect him? Maybe..." Laura stopped talking and wiped away the tears that were running down her cheeks. The thought of her father being in jail hurt her as much as losing Andy. "It's not your problem, Luca. It's not your problem," she whispered as she tried to hold back her tears.

"But I want to help."

"Right now, you can't help. No one can. Let's just be quiet, okay? Please?" Laura closed her eyes and sat back. She didn't know how to deal with her mixed emotions that were taking a roller-coaster ride. She felt angry, sad, frustrated, and mostly helpless. She also couldn't figure out the cell phone incident, the flashing images, and the weird feelings. She couldn't control or explain herself, and that added to her confusion. She wanted to push back the time before all this happened, before the accident. Before the accident that took away her brother and her father.

Why is this happening to me? Why did the accident happen? As the tears continued to roll down her face, she sat back and closed her eyes. Luca sat back in his seat too and glanced out the window opposite him. He, too, closed his eyes and fell asleep.

A half an hour later, Laura opened her eyes and looked out the window. The area was unfamiliar. The street sign read Charles Street. She noticed an empty lot filled with litter and a black-stained bathtub with a toilet seat inside it. The lot was the beginning of the area everyone termed as being unsafe. "The line of demarcation" as I. C. would say. The tree-lined houses, the park, the minimall, the stores, and her middle school were no longer in sight. She felt strong pangs in the pit of her stomach. She thought she was going to get sick.

"Luca, we have to get off." Laura pulled his sleeve.

"Okay, let's get off. Where are we?" Luca asked as soon as he opened his eyes.

"Nothing looks familiar." Luca looked out the window, as the bus continued on its route.

"Why did you fall asleep? Why didn't you wake me up? Now look at what you did! Is that how you help?"

"Laura, you told me to leave you alone, so I closed my eyes too. I didn't mean to fall asleep. I didn't think that you would fall asleep. You were so upset!"

"I didn't fall asleep...I sort of...I didn't sleep!" Laura noticed beads of perspiration on Luca's forehead and upper lip. Her hands felt clammy. She longed to see the stores, the park, and the tree-lined homes of her neighborhood with all its familiar faces and sights. The area was desolate. Litter and an empty lot surrounded the buildings. She swallowed and took a deep breath as she rubbed her clammy hands along the sides of her denim jeans.

"Let's get off at the next stop and take the other bus back. I hope you have enough money for the two of us. I only have eleven cents." Laura tried to sound calm.

"Where are we?" Luca asked again.

"We have to get off and turn around, Luca. We're on Charles Street." Laura clenched her teeth, barely getting Charles Street out of her mouth. "How much money do you have?"

"Okay, okay, calm down. I have money." Luca put his right hand in his right pocket to get his money. His fingers moved around inside the pocket, but he only felt the tips of what he knew were dimes. He put both hands in all the pockets he had in his jeans and winter jacket and quickly took them out.

"The ten-dollar bill, I don't have it. I put it in one of my pockets before I went out."

"Are you sure?" Laura asked.

"Yeah, I'm sure. I was going to use it to play the games at the mall. I put it in this pocket. I know I did." Luca's hand reached into his right jacket pocket again.

"You got it?" Laura asked anxiously.

"NO! I don't! I probably lost it." Luca turned pale.

Laura looked out the bus window. "Let's get off at the next stop. I'll figure out what to do." Laura was afraid, but she didn't want Luca to sense her fear. He had already turned paler than pale. They both got off, and Luca announced that it was beginning to rain.

"It's nothing," Laura remarked, trying to sound comforting. "There's the bus stop!" she shouted, pointing her finger to the sign across the street. Graffiti on the partly enclosed bus stop covered a poster. Laura was trying to figure out what the poster said but was only able to read some of the names of the graffiti artists who had left their marks. For an instant, she had forgotten the circumstances that brought her in front of the poster.

"Okay," she said, "this bus will take us back."

"How are we going to pay for the fares?"

"I don't know yet. Just give me a minute. I'll come up with something," Laura answered.

"Laura, it's beginning to rain, and we have no money for the bus. If my mom finds out that I ended up here, I'm grounded. We've got to get back. Let's walk back!" Luca's voice quivered.

"Walk back? Do you know how long that would take? And we don't have umbrellas."

"How are we going to get home? We can't just wait here."

"Look, I didn't ask you to come with me, right? You got on the bus all by yourself. I didn't force you." Laura felt her anger rising and was unable to control it.

"No, you didn't force me. I wanted to help you, and you…you blamed me for not waking you up…and…and did you check your pockets for money before you got on? Did you? Well, did you? I've had it with you, Laura. You've changed so much. I really don't think I want to be your friend anymore," Luca retaliated in a screeching loud voice.

"Sorry, Luca. I admit it. I didn't think." Luca turned away from Laura and stared at the poster. Laura's apology didn't make him feel any better. He wished that I. C. had been with them on their bus ride. He would have known what to do.

"Okay, Luca. Let's think. It's raining, and it will get dark soon, and we have no money." Laura bit her lower lip. She tried to state the facts just as she had seen a lawyer do on TV defending her client. "Now," she continued, "this is what we'll…we'll…just give me a minute. I'll come up with something." Laura turned her back to Luca and paced a few steps away from him. She took a deep breath and relaxed her shoulders. She thought and thought, but her mind was a complete blank, like an empty notebook page. She thought of the times she had stared at an empty page in her classroom after being given a writing assignment. Many times, those assignments had seemed impossible to begin, but she had always managed to complete them after the long blank period. Laura imagined that she was in her classroom once again faced with an assignment and another white blank sheet of paper. But nothing! She couldn't even think. Silent tears rolled down her cheeks. One tear rolled down to her lips. Her tongue brought it inside her mouth. The salty taste of the tiny drop added to her wounded pride.

"I'll call Jeff," Laura blurted out. Laura turned to Luca expecting a response, but instead she saw the same apparition she had seen in her room on Sunday night. As she gazed at her, more images flashed in front of her...flashes of the dreams, the feeling of floating in the air...and...and... transparent curved walls?

Laura thought she had gone mad. She closed her eyes and took a deep breath. When she opened her eyes, the apparition was gone. She turned around and saw Luca sitting on the edge of the sidewalk with his head buried in his lap.

"I'll call my brother. That's what I'll do. I'll ask him to come and get us."

"Great, Laura. Your brother doesn't have a license or have a car, remember?"

"Ronnie can drive him here. Yes, Ronnie has a car." Laura's words relieved her tension. "Ronnie has a car," she reiterated.

"What if he's not home? What if he can't reach her? What if..." Laura looked straight into Luca's frightened eyes.

"What if you just...oh no. I don't have a phone."

"What do you mean you don't have a phone? You always have a cell phone."

Laura lowered her head and sheepishly answered, "My mom took it away because she said I was...that bills were too high. She said that she gave me a cell phone to use for emergencies and not to use it so much and go over the minutes and...and...not to lose it. I lost two of them."

Luca thought he was going to faint. His knees felt weak, and his body went numb.

"This isn't happening. This isn't happening." He gasped for breath. "This isn't happening," he repeated. Luca's outbursts intensified Laura's fear.

"Stop it!" Laura screamed as loud as she could. "Do you have any change?" Luca nervously went through his pockets and found three dimes. "What good is this change, Laura?

"We can pay someone who comes along to use their cell."

As Laura desperately looked around, Luca called out in anguish, "This place is deserted. I'm going to be grounded till I'm eighteen years old!" Luca buried his head in his lap again.

Laura's eyes searched and searched, but there was no one in sight. She glanced at Luca and felt sorry for him. She knew she was responsible for being in this mess. She felt another tear and tried to wipe it off, but her hand couldn't move. She called for Luca, but her body shut down. She was frozen, a statue unable to move or utter a word. Her body suddenly rose from the ground and became suspended in midair. Laura was petrified, but the sudden appearance of the woman's face instantly comforted her. The woman was trying to help her, but her momentary feeling of relief left her as she watched in horror as another apparition, that of a hideous creature, was enveloping her with a translucent black veil. The covering pressed on her legs and was steadily inching up toward her chest. As it moved upward, the pressure increased. Laura knew that when it reached her chest, she'd stop breathing.

"Laura? Laura!" Luca screamed as loud as he could. "What's going on? What is that? Help! Somebody, help!" Luca cried out.

Laura watched motionless as Luca reached up and tried to pry open the veil that was crushing her. He scratched relentlessly with his bare hands to no avail. He sobbed and felt useless as he watched Laura slip away from him. But his call for help didn't go unheeded; Luca felt a tug as a gentle force pushed him to the ground and told him to lie still. It was the apparition of an elderly woman who telepathically told Luca that she was trying to save Laura. The apparition suddenly became vibrant, more defined. Laura watched as the hideous creature and the woman battled for her. The creature tried to envelope the woman with another veil, but it just melted away.

The creature pounced on the woman, but he went right through her. He wasn't as strong as the woman. The apparition faded in and out. The rain intensified, and as Luca shivered, he prayed that the woman would free Laura in time. The creature howled, faded in and out, and spun as he attempted to lift Laura away. The woman suddenly immersed Laura with a brilliant white light that made the creature howl louder than before. The bloodcurdling sounds made Luca cover his ears and close his eyes. He couldn't bear to watch. He wished that this was just a nightmare and that he'd soon wake up. The chilling screams stopped, and as he opened his eyes, the veil that had almost crushed Laura melted away; she was free.

"Laura, come here!" Luca yelled. Laura ran to Luca's side and watched in awe.

They heard the woman say, "You can't have her, Nnogarth. Give up. You're too weak, and you're no match for me now. I'm stronger than you." The apparition of the grotesque creature suddenly faded and disappeared.

Laura and Luca exchanged glances and then turned to the apparition.

"You saved her. Who are you?" Luca asked. The woman said nothing and immersed them with the same light that had enveloped Laura. A few moments later, they found themselves at the bus stop near their school.

"Luca?" Laura called out. "We're back at the bus stop. We're back at the bus stop," she repeated.

"Yes, we're back at the bus stop. Don't scare me like that again. I don't have any more money for us to go on another bus ride. We're back, so let's go home. Show that note to I. C. Maybe he can figure out who wrote it." Luca walked away from Laura.

"Luca, stop. I'm confused. How did we get here?"

"Laura, you're really scaring me now. Don't you remember? We got off at Charles Street. It took me all that time to talk you into coming back. Do you know how dangerous that part of town is? Do you know how...?"

Laura was not listening to Luca. She was immersed in her thoughts. *He doesn't know what happened. The woman, the horri-*

ble-looking creature, the white light—did I dream this? Laura quickly touched her clothing and looked at Luca's. They were dry.

"Luca, did we fall asleep on the bus?"

"No, Laura. Don't you remember what happened? You showed me the note, and you cried. I tried to tell you to ignore it, but you kept on crying and…Laura, you are freaking me out. Stop it. I have to get home. My mom is probably worried and will ground me till I'm eighteen if I don't get there now. Are you coming?" Luca lost his patience and walked ahead of Laura for a few moments. Laura thought she was going to get sick. She touched her face with her trembling hands that felt as hot as a summer beach day. Her anxiety worsened. She was convinced that she was going mad. She caught up to Luca, and they walked in silence to her house.

"Finally, you're home," Jeff called out from the kitchen, with Ronnie next to him. "How dare you make me worry about you? You know I'm responsible for you after school. Luca, where have you been?" Jeff continued. Luca was about to answer, but Laura spoke instead. She told Jeff that they took a bus ride to Charles Street and came back.

"Do you know how dangerous that place is? There's garbage there, broken-down buildings, empty lots filled with stuff…and… dangerous stuff…and…and…Luca, why on earth would you want to go there?"

"It wasn't his fault, Jeff. I went on the bus, and Luca tried to stop me, but I didn't listen…Please don't tell Mom. She's had it with me." Laura continued to plead with Jeff, but he wouldn't give in. Laura called him over and whispered in his ear. She told him that she saw him and Ronnie kissing on Sunday night and then winked at him. He threw his hands up in the air and looked up at the kitchen ceiling.

"Who invented sisters?" he asked as if he expected an answer.

"What just happened?" Ronnie was perplexed. Jeff gave her the "I'll tell you later look" and asked Luca if he wanted a ride home.

"Yeah, now…please," he pleaded.

They all got in the car to take Luca home. Laura sat back and relaxed. She thought about the events that had just occurred. It felt like a dream, and yet she knew it wasn't a dream. The incident frightened her, and not knowing what might happen next alarmed her even more. She glanced at Luca and wondered what he was thinking. Unlike her, he seemed calm, undisturbed. She tried not to think of it and distracted herself by looking out the window. Her eyes became fixed on the green bench that faced Centennial Bank, then Laura's body suddenly jolted. The woman whose face she had just seen on Charles Street appeared. She sat there, glanced at Laura, and vanished.

Who is she? No one sees her.

Laura's mind kept spinning with questions. She wanted to tell Luca and I. C, but she feared that they would not believe her. She decided that she would take a chance and tell Luca. They had been friends for such a long time; he might believe her. She would speak to him tomorrow.

"Are you going to tell Mom on me? About the kiss, I mean?" Jeff asked Laura as soon as they walked back into the house.

"No, and you're not going to tell Mom about the bus ride, about going to Charles Street. Deal?"

"Mom should know that..."

"Jeff, do we have a deal?" Laura interrupted.

"Yeah, I guess so. We're even."

Chapter 7

The next day, Laura spoke to Luca in private as I. C. stopped by the library to check out a book. She told him that what she was about to tell him had to remain a secret between them.

"Do you swear that you won't tell anyone, not even I. C., about what happened?"

"Laura, you're gonna make me swear, and then you're gonna accuse me of not keeping my promise, right? So why should I even bother?"

"Just swear you won't tell. This is important." Laura stared into Luca's light-brown eyes and waited for an answer.

"Only if you're not gonna accuse—"

"Oh, cut that out," Laura interrupted.

"Okay, I swear I won't tell…not even…not even I. C., my best friend," Luca reluctantly added.

Laura gave Luca all the details and hoped that he'd believe her.

"Come on, Laura. You can't be serious. You probably just imagined it, or…"

"I heard her, and I saw her face." Laura stopped for a moment and continued, "It's weird, but I know what happened, and she helped me…and then fought with that horrible creature that almost …killed me…I couldn't breathe…because…you know…" Laura stammered. She felt her chest getting tighter and tighter as if it were happening again. She took a deep breath, continued her story, but stopped mid-sentence. "Okay, okay. Luca, *you* tell me what happened."

"When we got off the bus, you pointed to the bus stop across the street, and we took the very next bus that came along. We almost freaked out when we saw where we were. It's a good thing I had money with me because you only had some change that wasn't enough for the bus fare." Laura was beside herself.

"Okay, okay." Laura's voice quivered.

"Are you feeling okay, Laura?"

Laura's mind raced with doubts and unexplainable events; she was speechless. She stood in front of Luca and went into a trance.

"Laura...Laura," Luca called out. "You look awful."

"What?"

"Maybe we should ask I. C. He may know what happened to you," Luca suggested.

"No, we're not asking I. C. What can he do? Is he going to look it up in one of his thick psychology books? Or...Or...do endless searches on his computer? We're not asking anyone. You hear? We're not asking anyone, not even I. C." Laura's voice quivered again. "I'm going home." Laura walked ahead of Luca and tried to hold back her tears.

"Aren't you gonna wait for I. C.?" Luca asked.

"Yeah, I was, but I'd rather go home."

"Are you gonna take another bus to somewhere?"

"I should've never told you. I knew you wouldn't believe me. I'm going." Laura felt worse than before.

"Laura!" Luca yelled as she quickly walked away. "Fine, go home. Go find your ghost. See if I care." Luca thought about his friend. He wondered when all this was going to go away...when was she going to act like her old self. They used to have fun together. He wanted to tell I. C., but he was of two minds; he had promised Laura he wouldn't.

Chapter 8

The following day, all three of them were on their way to the mall to play their favorite video games. Luca told his version of the story to I. C. "And Ronnie took me home," ended Luca.

"Weren't you scared?" I. C. asked, turning to Laura.

"I was," added Luca. "It was getting late, and I would've had to face my mom. But I got home just in time."

"Why did you go on that bus? You took off without a plan and without money. You were very impulsive. I certainly would have given it a lot of thought. And I wouldn't have taken such a risk," I. C. said.

Laura looked at I. C. and pointed her finger back and forth between her and him. "That's the difference between us. You think too much, and I act without all that thinking!"

I. C. turned Laura's finger away from his face, held on to it, and said sarcastically, "I'd still rather be safe than sorry, Ms....Ms.... uh..."

"Ms. who?" asked Laura. "Who are you going to compare me to, one of your science-fiction creatures from one of your books? Well? Are you?" She was more frightened and nervous than she led I. C. to believe. A cold chill swept her body as the apparition of the ugly creature paralyzed her thoughts.

"Speaking of science-fiction characters and creatures, have you read the book about Captain Nemo?" No one answered I. C., so he rambled on about the book he was reading.

"Have you heard of *Twenty Thousand Leagues Under the Sea*? It's one of Verne's best works. The main character is Captain Nemo." I. C. turned to Luca and asked, "Do you want me to tell you about the spooky captain?"

"Captain who?" Luca sheepishly asked.

"Captain Nemo, the main character."

"I don't know. I guess." Luca shrugged his shoulders and looked at Laura.

"Well, I don't want to know about some nutty captain," Laura interjected. She wanted to sound normal. "I have more important things that I want to know about."

Luca glanced at Laura and was about to speak when Laura elbowed him. Luca ignored Laura's signal to stop and said, "Tell him, Laura. Tell him." Laura elbowed Luca again and motioned him to stop. I. C. waited with anticipation to hear what Laura had to say, but Laura said nothing. The threesome continued their walk to the video arcade in silence. I. C. wondered what Luca had wanted Laura to share with him. Despite Laura's reluctance to speak, he knew that eventually Luca would tell him.

On their way back from the mall, Laura almost tripped over something that felt like a big thick stick. There, right in front of her was the brown cane that belonged to the woman she had been thinking about.

"Sorry," Laura said as she regained her balance.

It's her!

"Are you all right?" asked the woman as Laura picked up the cane and returned it to her in an upright position.

"I guess I was daydreaming," Laura answered.

"I'm so sorry my cane interrupted your thoughts. I hope they were of a happy nature," the elderly woman said, smiling.

"Sort of. I'm not sure," Laura said softly, almost in a whisper. Laura kept staring at her, not sure what she should say next. The boys, who had been a few steps ahead of Laura, turned around and walked back toward her.

"What's going on?" asked Luca.

"Oh, it's Mrs....Mrs...." I. C. snapped his fingers three times as he tried to remember the woman's name. He then realized that the woman hadn't ever mentioned her name.

"I'm Lily. Yes, we have met before, haven't we, Leopold?" she said, smiling at I. C.

"I hate that name." I. C. put both hands over his ears. Luca burst out laughing as he watched I. C.'s reaction. Laura watched I. C. converse with the woman, who now had a name. She wanted to continue the conversation they had started before the boys had arrived.

"Where do you live?" Laura blurted out.

"A block away from the bank, next to the C&D Deli."

I. C. and Luca watched the two females. They listened as they moved their heads from side to side as if they were watching a tennis match. Luca elbowed I. C. several times, as he tried to take part in the conversation.

"Why is she spending so much time speaking to the old woman?" I. C. asked Luca.

"I guess she likes her," Luca responded.

"How did she know my real name?" I. C. asked Luca again. Luca shrugged his shoulders and glanced at Laura and her new friend.

"Are you coming, Laura?" Luca called out.

"No, guys, I'll catch up with you in a little while." Laura's eyes did not move from Lily's face as she spoke.

"See ya!" Luca hollered.

"You have a lot of questions, don't you, Laura?" Lily asked.

"I do...but...uh..." Laura stammered. She felt flushed. Her face was burning. She looked away from Lily and stared at the ground. She focused on a candy wrapper littering the pavement. Her hands trembled as she picked it up and stood in front of Lily with the wrapper in her right hand.

"When Luca and I were at Charles Street, you saved me from that monster, that creature who almost...and...uh...what...who was he?" Laura was too nervous to continue and couldn't finish her sentence. She sat down, lowered her head, and mumbled, "Am I losing my mind? Only crazy people see weird things and hear voices."

Lily extended her hand toward Laura's chin and lifted it until their eyes met. "Laura, listen to me. You did see me. I had to help you. It's part of the plan."

"What plan are you talking about?"

"All this will make sense at another time. For now, it's important for you to know that you are being helped. I'm here to see to it."

"What about my father...My father...he's gone. He had to leave us. The accident happened because of me...and...everyone is saying that he's in jail...and...Andy...Andy is still missing." Laura paced back and forth as the anger welled up inside her. The more she paced, the angrier she became. Her anger was like a dark cloud that was about to explode and allow all the water to gush out. Laura's throat tightened. The words just wouldn't come out. The more she tried, the tighter her throat became. She finally burst into tears and gave up the effort to speak.

"I know about Andy and the reason your father left."

"How?" Laura could barely whisper.

"When it's time, everything will be clear to you. You need to be patient till then. Your father is being helped. I'm here to help you."

"I don't need help!" Laura's anger took over. Lily's body began to change. As it transformed, a brilliant white light immersed Laura in its splendor. Laura's body began to tingle, and then it became numb. It was the same feeling she'd had when one of her feet had fallen asleep. Her whole body felt like one big foot that had fallen asleep. And then Lily spoke, "You need to learn the truth. Close your eyes and watch." Laura did as she was told. As her eyes closed, she saw a vision of her father. He was in the driver's seat, and Andy was sitting in the back, safely strapped to his seat. Laura calmly watched the scene of the accident unfold before her. As the images appeared one after the other, Laura felt as if she were in her living room watching a movie. She watched without any emotions, as Lily protected her with her light. Laura watched her father's car being hit by a driver who had passed a red light. She saw the collision that hit the right rear side of the car where Andy sat. Her father tried to avoid the crash by speeding away from the oncoming vehicle, but the other car was going too fast. The hideous creature that had attacked her suddenly appeared and snatched Andy away. The images stopped.

"No, don't stop. I want to see more," Laura called out.

"This is all you need to see about the accident, but there is something else for you to know." Laura watched the events that led Lily to take her to the bubble on the two occasions when Laura had been in grave danger. She understood why she couldn't explain Jeff's phone in her backpack. She also understood that Lily had saved her life many times.

"I was able to transport you to the bubble to heal your body, Laura, but you also need to heal from within." Laura did not listen to Lily. Her mind was on other things.

"If you can do all that, why can't you help me find who started the rumors? Why can't you bring Andy back? Why can't you bring back my father?"

"You have to stop using your energy to that end, Laura. You have to control your anger. Your quest for revenge will endanger your life. You must let it go."

"I need to know. Please help me," Laura pleaded.

"I can't stay any longer. I'm beginning to fade."

Laura opened her eyes and felt the numbness slowly leaving. The tingling came back, and when that was gone, she was able to move. She looked around for Lily, but she was not there.

"She's gone. She's gone—she did it again," Laura mumbled to herself. "No one is ever going to believe this," she said out loud. Laura marveled at Lily's extraordinary abilities, but she couldn't understand why she refused to help her. Lily's pleas went unheeded, as Laura was still intent on finding the person responsible for starting the rumors.

Chapter 9

I t was a sunny day to be outdoors, even though it was cold. Laura and the boys were walking home from school. Groups of threes and fours walked close to them. Some groups passed them by; others leisurely walked behind them and in front of them.

"Why is Jill covering her mouth as she's talking to Lisa?" Laura asked Luca.

"I don't know," Luca answered.

"Maybe she has a case of halitosis," I. C. said, giggling.

"Here he goes, using a word that only he knows," complained Luca.

"Look at her. Now she's looking at me and covering her mouth. She doesn't have hala…hale…whatever I. C. said. She's got a bad case of talking about me!" Laura exclaimed and walked toward the group of girls.

"Are you talking about me?" Laura asked Jill.

"What makes you think that?" Jill answered in a shrill tone.

"Well, maybe because you kind of covered your mouth and stared at me while you were blabbing to Lisa, that's why," Laura answered, mimicking Jill's tone.

"I wasn't talking about you!" Jill continued to tease Laura.

"Then who were you talking about?" Laura asked louder than before.

"It's none of your business, and move out of my way." Jill put her hand between Laura's body and hers and motioned her to make a path.

"I'm not moving until you talk!" Laura screamed. "I thought you were my friend. Why are you acting like that?"

"Laura, let's go. Leave her alone," Luca called out and grabbed Laura's arm.

"If you must know, we were talking about your father. Everyone knows that he got drunk and caused the accident, and he is a coward. He did nothing to stop the kidnappers from taking your brother. He's a drunken coward." Lisa spit out the words to Laura's face.

"And now he's in jail, where he belongs," added Jill.

"That's not true, you liar. How dare you talk about my father!" Laura yelled. "The other driver passed a red light and crashed into my father… And he wasn't drinking. You started these lies. You're supposed to be my friend." Laura repeated as she inched her body closer to Jill and pointed her finger at her face.

"Laura, let's go," Luca called out again and pulled her back.

"Oh, look, Lisa, she's got a bodyguard," Jill called out. "Luca is her bodyguard."

"I don't need someone to fight my battles. I'll punch your big mouth so hard you'll never tell a lie again." Laura pulled her arm away from Luca and threw herself at Jill. Both girls dropped their books and started hitting aimlessly. Jill's right fist somehow found its way to Laura's nose. Laura swung back but missed her target. She felt another blow on her face. The impact forced Laura to fall back and land on Luca. Both fell backward, as Luca lost his balance. I. C. ran to Laura and helped her get on her feet.

"Don't worry about me. Run after those two. Jill punched me," she wailed. "Twice!" she yelled with pain.

I. C. ignored Laura's demands and continued to help her get up on her feet.

"I can't believe she punched you. Oh no! Laura, you're bleeding!" Luca pointed to the blood that was dripping on Laura's chin. Some drops had already dripped on her sneakers.

"I bet she started the rumors about my father. I bet she did. I just know she did, the creep."

"Right now, you need help. Let's take her to her house, I. C." Luca tried to comfort Laura.

"Why didn't you run after them, I. C.?" Laura shouted.

"You wanted me to run after a couple of girls?" he answered in a huff.

"Never mind, I. C., never mind. I'll get even. I'll get even. You'll see."

Luca and I. C. held on to Laura as they walked her to her house. Laura opened the door and rushed to the bathroom. She found some tissues and put them inside her nostril as the boys watched her. She continued to mumble about getting revenge.

"What should we do, I. C.?" Luca asked. "Her nose is swollen."

"Ice. When in doubt, apply ice." Luca took some ice from the freezer and wrapped it in paper towels.

"Ouch!" Laura moved the ice pack away from her nose.

"Laura, you do it," Luca cried. Laura took the ice pack and put it on her nose.

"What time will your mom be home?" I. C. asked.

"She's pobaly shoing the new condos tothday. She's usually home by sis," Laura mumbled. She tried to continue talking, but I. C. told her not to and motioned Luca to make another ice pack.

"Hold this on your eye, Laura." Luca put the other ice pack in Laura's right hand and directed it to her left eye.

"I'm going to get even with her!"

"Your mom should call Jill's house, and Jill's mom is the one who should take care of this," I. C. said reassuringly.

"No, she'll just keep on talking about my father. She won't do anything!" Laura started to cry.

"It's just a rumor that your father is in jail because of the accident. People just like to talk. Don't pay any attention to it. You know it's not true. Don't waste your energy on that, Laura. Let Jill's mother take care of it." I. C.'s comforting words did not make Laura feel better.

Laura removed the ice pack blocking her mouth and screamed, "She started it. I know she did!"

"Calm down, Laura. Your nose may start to bleed again," Luca cried. No one spoke for a while. Luca wondered how Laura was going to get even with Jill, and I. C. wondered why Laura was unable to defend herself. He had expected Jill to go home with the bloody nose, not Laura.

Laura removed the ice pack from her eye and suddenly gasped. "Guys, do you see what I see?" she whispered.

"What's Lily doing here?" Luca mumbled to I. C. in amazement.

"She just appeared." I. C. choked on his words. "But...but...how?"

"It's happened before. You see, Luca, that's what happened at Charles Street. She just appeared there too. I told you it happened. Now do you believe me?" Laura dropped both ice packs and went closer to Lily.

"They can see you. They see you," she repeated.

"Look what happened to Laura." I. C. pointed to Laura's face.

"What happened, Laura?" Lily asked. I. C. and Luca took turns relating the story to Lily as Laura kept mumbling that she was going to get even. Lily called Laura and motioned for her to sit next to her. Laura obeyed. Lily looked at Laura's swollen face. She began speaking in her soft, soothing voice. "Laura, forget about the revenge that you have in mind."

"I can't do that. She told everyone in school that my father caused the accident and that he's in jail." Laura cried. Her tears mixed with the blood from her nose that began to bleed again. The tears in Laura's eyes clouded her sight as well as her memories of Lily.

"I feel your pain, Laura, but you must let go of your anger."

"You don't understand," Laura cried out.

Lily did not speak again. She stood up. Her body illuminated and immersed Laura's face with resplendent white light. Laura felt her body tingle just as it had done before. She expected to feel numb, and she did. She knew that the numbness would be followed by her inability to move. This time, however, she didn't know what to expect next. Laura stopped crying, and before everyone's eyes, her face healed. The boys were astounded. They walked around Laura as they examined her face. Laura carefully touched her face with her long slender fingers. She touched her nose and the eye that had just been swollen and painful to the very same touch. Only Laura heard Lily say that the healing would be completed on the Enchanted Carousel. Lily's message did not register in Laura's mind. All she could say was, "You see, Luca, this is what I was talking about. Now do you believe me?"

"You've experienced this before? When? Where?" I. C. shrieked. "How did she do that?" I. C. behaved as the intellectual and curious individual that he was and continued to ask more questions. Laura turned to Lily. Lily gestured that it was okay for her to speak about their previous encounters. The boys listened to Laura's stories so intently that they didn't notice that Lily had faded away.

"And then I saw how my dad tried to avoid the accident and what happened to Andy," Laura said, ending her story.

"She's gone!" Luca announced.

"She did it again!" Laura shrieked as she touched her healed face over and over.

I. C. darted toward the front door, murmuring as he looked around for Lily. "She even knows my real name. Who is she? A magician. She's probably a magician. Magicians create illusions. Yes, that's what it was, an illusion."

"What are you going to tell your mom? Are you going to tell her about the fight and Lily?" Luca whispered.

"No! She won't believe me. Did *you* believe me at first?"

"Uh…" Luca threw his hands up in the air and asked, "How can anyone believe this without seeing it?"

"Well, now you know I was telling you the truth. Both of you know," she said louder.

"Are you going to tell your mom about the fight?" I. C. asked.

"Yeah, well, Jill's mother might call. What do you think?"

"Maybe you should tell her in case she does call. Your mom would want to hear it from you first."

"How are you going to get even with Jill?" Luca changed the subject.

"Oh…she'll pay. You'll see."

"Whatever you decide to do, she'll deserve it." Luca paused and then slowly walked toward the door.

"I've got to go. See you tomorrow. Are you coming, Leopold?" Luca giggled.

"Stop calling me that hideous name. I'll see you, Laura," I. C. answered. As the boys were leaving, Mrs. Stephens came through the door.

"Hi, Luca. Hi, I. C."

"Hi, Mrs. Stephens," the boys said together.

"We were just leaving," I. C. said.

"So long, boys. Regards to your parents."

Chapter 10

That night, Mrs. Stephens announced that she wanted to speak to her children. For a moment, Laura thought that she might have found out about the fight, but she was relieved to hear that her mom had other issues to discuss.

"Laura, Jeff, I spoke to your father about how I'd like the three of us to go back to some of the routines that we had before…before the accident. I think it might be good for us."

Laura wanted to blurt out what she had learned from Lily about the accident and about the creature that had snatched Andy away, but she had no voice. She couldn't speak. She was exploding inside.

"What did you have in mind, Mom?" Jeff spoke first.

Laura tried to listen as they spoke, but the voices seemed far away as she tried to make sense of what they were saying.

"Let's give it a try. To start, I'm going to be home from work at 4:30. I'll show homes during the day and do the paperwork at night. And how about going back to having pizza together on Friday nights? We can start that tomorrow."

"I guess it's okay," muttered Jeff. "But I can still go out after, right?"

"Yes, Jeff." She quickly turned to Laura and said, "You can have your sleepovers again, Laura." Mrs. Stephens turned to her daughter. Laura looked down at the kitchen table, avoiding the two sets of eyes that were waiting for a response. She suddenly heard herself say, "I don't have any girlfriends, so the sleepovers don't matter." Laura lowered her eyes again. *Strange*, she thought. Those thoughts had a voice but not what she really wanted to confess…that she knew about the accident and Andy.

Mrs. Stephens was puzzled by Laura's response but continued, "We're all in this together, Laura." Mrs. Stephens looked at her children and then at Andy's place at the table. She stared at the empty seat and then covered her face with both hands to cover her teary eyes. Laura didn't expect her mom to openly display her pain. She hadn't cried in front of them since their life-changing event.

"How can we eat dinner together and look at Andy's empty chair? I know that we should try, but maybe…" Jeff couldn't finish his thought.

Mrs. Stephens looked up as Jeff spoke and said, "No, I already discussed it with your father. The longer we postpone it, the worse it will get. We'll begin tomorrow. I'll order the pizza at about six, and we'll all have dinner together. Laura, you haven't said a thing."

"Mom," Laura whispered out loud. Mrs. Stephens turned to Laura's direction and waited. But Laura just looked at her, unable to continue.

"Did you want to say something?"

Laura bit her upper lip and looked down. Jeff took one glance at Laura and left to watch the news in the living room.

"You might get a call from Jill's mom." Laura still avoided eye contact.

"Why? Is she planning on moving? Does she want me to look for a house?" Mrs. Stephens paused and then said, "Are you upset because Jill is moving away?" The notion of Jill moving lifted Laura's spirits for an instant.

"That would take care of one of the creeps," Laura muttered to herself.

"What did you say?"

"Uh…It's not what you think. It's worse." Laura sighed very loudly. "Okay, here goes." Laura spoke as fast as a speeding train trying to cheat time. "Jill started an argument with me, and we got into a fight after school."

"You don't mean an actual fight, uh…a fistfight, do you?"

Laura nodded.

"Laura, look at me." Laura looked up and stared at the kitchen painting she had stared at many times before and still thought that it was ugly. Mrs. Stephens inspected Laura's face and her arms and legs and finally asked, "Did you hurt her?"

"No, she's fine. I think."

"Are you hurt? Did she hit you?"

"Yes, uh...well, no!"

"What do you mean, Laura? Are you or are you not hurt?" her mother demanded to know.

"I thought I was, but I'm not." Laura was so confused she didn't know what to say or how to say it without mentioning Lily. "Look, Mom, see?" Laura put her body in front of her mother for further inspection. "I'm fine."

"Tell me what happened." Mrs. Stephens told Laura to sit down. Both of them sat down as Laura told her the story exactly as it happened with the exception of the bloody nose and swollen eye. She did tell her that she fell down and that was what had made her suspect that she had gotten hurt.

"Why couldn't you just walk away from them? You know better."

"How could I just listen to them talk about us, about Daddy?"

"What exactly did she say that caused the fight?"

"Jill said that Daddy was drunk and caused the...and...that he's in...in...jail."

"Laura, you know that's not true. I've tried to explain to you what happened. You saw your father that night, and you saw how he looked and how proud he was of you."

"Why did he leave us? Why did he run away?" Laura could no longer control her emotions. Her doubts haunted her. Her mother attempted to put her arms around her and again explain the circumstances that led to his absence, but Laura pulled away and fled up the stairs to her room.

"What's going on?" Jeff asked as he came into the kitchen.

"Laura got into a fight with Jill."

"Who won?" Jeff jokingly asked. Mrs. Stephens glared at Jeff and said nothing.

"Just kidding, Mom." Jeff's tone of voice changed. "Did anyone get hurt?" he continued.

"Apparently not," Mrs. Stephens answered.

"What was the fight about?" Jeff asked. Mrs. Stephens told him what Laura had just narrated to her and asked him if he knew about the nasty rumors. Jeff said that he wasn't aware of the gossip and that it probably was a girl thing. He defended his sister's actions and remarked that he would have reacted the same way.

"Why would Jill say such cruel things?" Jeff didn't know what to say. Deep in thought, he realized how much his sister was hurting. He understood why she had been acting so mean. After a few moments, he responded, "It's gossip, Mom. Just gossip."

"Gossip hurts, and it's hurting your sister. It's hurting us. So that's why Laura said she had no girlfriends. Lisa must be involved in this too," she added.

"Mom, it'll go away. You'll see."

"Soon, I hope…soon."

Laura sat on her bed and thought about Andy. She knew that she would see him again. She knew that Lily would rescue him. She missed her little brother. She recalled the funny things that he did and how his sense of adventure had irritated her at the time. She opened the desk drawer and took out a picture of Andy celebrating his sixth birthday. Laura stared at the picture with longing eyes. Perhaps if she stared at Andy long enough, the picture might come to life and Andy would suddenly appear.

Chapter 11

I t was a gloomy Friday; the air felt heavy. It had rained through the night, and the dark clouds blocked the light that gave day-time its brilliance. The sun tried to make an appearance, but the clouds firmly stood their ground. It was drizzling as Laura walked the four blocks to I. C.'s house for an after-school reunion with the boys. The raindrops spotted Laura's blue jeans and sneakers. She walked toward the front door with the sign The Williams Family. Mrs. Williams, a tall African American woman in her forties, quickly opened the door when she peeked through the blinds and saw Laura standing in the rain. After greetings were exchanged, Mrs. Williams brought a towel to her young guest to dry her face and the top of her head. She remarked that it was getting nasty outside and had better get her shopping done before the weather got worse. She escorted Laura to the family room, where the boys were already having a snack, and went out. Laura walked toward them with the wet towel in her hands. She immediately howled and covered her ears at the sound of the blaring music.

"What are you listening to?" she sputtered and threw herself on the soft cushions of the sofa.

"To something you obviously don't like," I. C. said as he sat next to her.

"I've never heard it before." The wailing electric guitar solo that dominated the tune strangely reminded her of the terrible experience she had on Charles Street. Her body shook as she dried her hair.

"Well, brace yourself. The next piece is very similar."

Laura covered her ears. "Ah-h-h-hu-ah-ah," she screeched. "I never would've guessed you like this stuff. It's just not like you."

"You're right. It's not." I. C. turned off the music.

"Have a snack, Laura." Luca offered a toasted English muffin topped with tomato sauce and mozzarella cheese.

"My mom just made these," I. C. said with his mouth full.

"Minipizza, my favorite." Luca reached for another one. The word *pizza* reminded Laura of something she thought her mother had said but couldn't recall what it was. The thought made her nervous, unsettled. She gazed at the window being pounded by the rain. Her eyes followed one raindrop. As it landed on the glass, it made a tiny splash, and then it rolled down and united with another one. The new creation was larger and heavier. Its weight caused it to break and splatter down to the bottom of the windowpane.

"Want something to drink?" Laura had begun to focus on another drop to see if it would meet a similar fate but lost sight of it. She turned to him and asked him what he had and he replied, "There's coke, coke, and there's coke."

"Well, I think I'll have a coke." Laura and I. C. amused each other.

"One coke coming up." I. C. went to the kitchen to get the beverage as Luca and Laura walked to the bookshelves that were from floor to ceiling. They searched for the paper marker I. C. left on the fourth shelf that recorded the number of books he had read in the past week. The marker had two numbers. The top number represented the last count of books I. C. had read; the bottom was the new count.

"139 plus eight. That makes 147," I. C. called out as he came back with Laura's coke.

"You read eight books in seven days? You're such a nerd," Luca teased I. C.

Laura walked around the boys to see which books he read. She read some of the titles to herself. *The Great Houdini, Magic, The World of Illusions, Twenty Thousand Leagues Under the Sea, Bodybuilding,* and *Body Fitness.*

As they ate their snacks, Laura anxiously waited for them to finish their seconds so they could discuss what they were going to do that afternoon. Laura had her own plans though. She wanted to talk about how she was going to get even with Jill and Lisa. The realization that her friends had started the rumor hurt her immensely. She walked around the family room muttering to herself at first and then lamented loudly to the boys.

"I thought they liked me? What did I do to them?" She had imagined that it had been someone she casually knew, someone who didn't care about her. But her friends? That was hard to accept. Laura hit the sofa pillows with her fists as she let out some of her anger.

"Why? Why?" she repeatedly asked. In an awkward move to get up from the sofa, Laura tripped and lost her balance. As she fell down, her head hit the corner of the side table near the sofa. She lay on the floor with her eyes closed and did not move.

"She hit her head!" Luca screamed. "Laura, are you all right?"

"Laura, can you hear me?" I. C. knelt down next to her.

"She's not moving. I. C., get your mother...get...get somebody...get your mother."

"You know she's not home. She went to the supermarket...at... the supermarket in the mall!" I. C. shrieked.

"She's not moving! Laura...Laura, are you okay?" Luca yelled in horror. "I'm calling 911... she's...she's unconscious. Why does everything happen to her! Why?"

I. C. ran to the phone and picked up the receiver.

"Wait," Luca hollered. "Did you see that? Lightning had just struck near the house."

"That rarely happens in the winter," I. C. cried out.

"Look, I. C." Luca pointed at something.

"What *is* going on?" He turned around and slowly put the receiver down as he gazed at the wondrous sight. Lily was hovering above Laura's lifeless body. They saw the familiar brilliant white light from Lily's body immerse Laura. The fear in the boys' eyes vanished as they watched in awe. Laura moved and opened her eyes. She smiled at Lily and held out her arms. The boys sighed in relief and waited for Laura to get up, but Laura's body was as still as a statue.

In midair, Lily's appearance kept changing—old Lily, young Lily, old Lily, young Lily. The images kept flashing like a blinking red light.

"What on earth is going on?" Luca choked. "Look at Lily. Is that what she really looks like? She's old and young at the same time."

"Could it have been the strange occurrence of the lightning?" I. C. asked. "I did see lightning. It probably struck Lily. That's when everything stopped, and she began to change from young to old. Something went wrong. It had to be the lightning," I. C. said authoritatively and answered his own question.

Thunder was heard at a distance.

"Thunder too? That's rare in the winter months, but possible, I guess," I. C. exclaimed. "The thunderstorm is moving away from here," I. C. continued.

Laura's arms were still stretched out, and Lily was still in metamorphosis. "Do you think they're gonna stay like this forever?" Luca's eyes were still fixed on the two figures suspended in time.

"Don't even think that. Something must have happened…It's… the lightning. I think the lightning blocked Lily in some way. It must have affected her power. That's the only thing that I can think of."

"What's that sound?" Luca was almost afraid to ask. Before I. C. could answer, they heard Lily's voice.

"Nnogarth…she's mine. Leave her alone! You can't stop me."

"What is that?" Luca was horrified.

I. C. stared at the creature in disbelief and cried out, "Lily, he's going after Laura!"

The grotesque face with an indistinguishable body appeared above Laura's outstretched arms. He had tried to abduct her when she and Luca were on Charles Street. The apparition had been yanked and then sucked away as if by a vacuum cleaner. Lily's half-lit transparent body replaced the hideous creature. As Lily got closer to Laura, the ugly creature appeared again and pounced on Lily. The struggle between the two intertwined images bounced off the walls of the room as the boys moved around with them. At times, it seemed as if Lily was losing the fight, but she kept coming back with more power and energy. The creature's howls got louder, and a face took form and became bigger and bigger. Lily fought for Laura, but a violent blow made her bounce several times from the ceiling to the floor, to the wall, and then catapulted to the ground. As she landed on the floor, Lily's form changed again from young to old and old to young. It became obvious to the boys that Lily was losing and the hideous creature was winning the battle for Laura. Lily's transparent body totally faded away. As the boys watched in terror, the creature made another horrific sound as he enveloped Laura with the black translucent veil. Lily reappeared and materialized in flesh and bones this time. She immersed Laura with a bright white light and freed her from Nnogarth's grasp. Laura lay on the floor, still unconscious. The appearance of the white light frightened Nnogarth, and he instantly disappeared. Lily sat down and tried to speak, but she couldn't. It seemed that freeing Laura took all her energy away. She glanced at Laura, and she, too, disappeared.

Luca finally had the courage to speak. "What are we supposed to do *now?*"

I. C. could not answer. He walked around aimlessly with his hands on his head trying to find a solution. Luca kept on talking and asking questions. "I don't know what's going on, but at least Lily got Laura back from that...that thing, that creature, whatever it was. But Laura is still not moving. What do we do now, I. C.?" Luca screamed. "We almost lost both of them...both of them. We have to get Lily back. What if he comes back for us?"

"He doesn't want us. He wants Laura," I. C. quickly answered.

"What does he want with her? Why does he want her?" Luca bellowed. I. C. didn't answer. He was lost in his thoughts.

"I don't know, but it's obvious he only wanted Laura. He didn't come after us. But now we have to get Lily back so she can help Laura." I. C. sighed.

"Yeah, but that thing might come back too," Luca exclaimed.

"How do we get Lily back?" I. C. asked out loud, ignoring Luca's concern.

"Don't you think Lily will come back to help Laura again? She always appears when Laura is in trouble." Luca's voice quivered.

"Maybe this winter thunderstorm might prevent her from coming back. You saw what happened earlier. Lightning is dangerous for her…and now that ugly thing…I'm sure she wants to come back to help Laura. We can't help her. Maybe we should call 911." I. C.'s thoughts were all over the place.

"Lily, please come back," Luca called out.

Lightning struck again. Both boys froze in fear, knowing that Lily could not return while the storm lingered. To their amazement, Lily did appear; but just like before, Lily's form changed from young to old and old to young. She quickly faded as she got closer to Laura.

"Did you see that? I knew she'd be back," Luca screeched. "And I didn't hear any weird sounds. Did you?"

"No, but Laura is still unconscious. Lily tried to come back but…Wait!" I. C. screamed. "I think the lightning helps Lily, *not* harm her. Lightning just struck, and Lily tried to reappear. Maybe she needs more power." I. C. paced back and forth as he tried to figure out how to help Lily. He muttered to himself for a few moments and then announced, "That's it! I…I think that's it. Thunderstorms in the winter are rare, so…so…she must have created the thunderstorm! Of course, that's the only explanation. We have to help her by giving her more energy, more electricity, now…before that monster gets here," I. C. answered.

"How?"

"Let's see. Lightning is electricity. We need to create electricity. If I'm right…if I'm right…I hope I'm right…we can get Lily back."

"And if you're wrong?" Luca yelled.

"Do you have a better idea?" I. C. yelled back.

"How are you going to create lightning?" Luca's eyes practically bulged from their sockets.

"Not create lightning. Create an electrical shock. We need to create electricity and shock her." I. C. paced back and forth again.

"You want to electrocute Lily?"

"Yeah, I just hope that's the answer." I. C. stopped pacing. "I have an idea. Put some water in the largest bowl you can find in the kitchen, and I'll get a hair dryer. Go on!"

Luca did as he was told and returned with a large bowl of water.

"Put the bowl here where we last saw Lily." I. C. pointed to the spot where Lily had faded away. "Give me the hairdryer." I. C.

plugged in the hairdryer. "When I throw in the hair dryer in the bowl, it will create a spark of electricity. I hope the electrical shock is strong enough."

"You're going to electrocute Lily?" Luca asked again. His mouth remained open.

"Yup." I. C. seemed confident. "It's not high enough. We have to put the bowl on a chair." I. C. got a chair and placed the bowl on it. "Move away. Here goes!" I. C. turned the switch on and threw the hair dryer in the water. Sparks of electricity flashed what seemed to be images of Lily.

"Did you see that? Lily's trying to come back," hollered I. C. The room illuminated like a dark sky lit by fireworks. Blue, red, and yellow beams of light bounced off the walls, and then Lily's image spiraled down from the ceiling and became suspended in midair. Lily's transparent body began to change: young Lily, old Lily, young, old. The images changed back and forth.

"OH NO!" Luca screamed. "We killed her!"

I. C. stared at the flashing lights and cried out, "NO, NO, LILY. COME BACK. LILY, YOU HAVE TO HELP LAURA!"

"Let's throw in the toaster. She needs more electricity." Luca ran to the kitchen and returned with the toaster. I. C. grabbed it from him, plugged it in, and threw it in the water too. More sparks flew, and Lily reappeared. As the two boys stared in awe, Lily's apparition merged, and the two images of Lily became one. The old Lily the boys knew remained solid and intact.

"YES!" both boys cried out.

"It worked, I. C. It worked! I'll never call you a nerd again!"

Lily immediately immersed Laura in her splendid light, and Laura awoke.

"You're okay...Yes!" I. C. exclaimed.

"You're back," Luca blurted out, relieved.

"What happened?" Laura asked very calmly. "Why was I on the floor? Wait." She held out her hand. The boys didn't have a chance to respond. "Now I remember. I fell."

"Don't you remember anything else?" Luca asked.

"I remember that I fell, and I had a horrible dream."

Luca gave a detailed explanation of the extraordinary events they had just witnessed.

"Lily was here?" Laura touched her head but felt nothing out of the ordinary. The three children looked for Lily, but she was gone.

"We thought you were dead," I. C. said.

Luca and I. C. looked at each other and then looked at the spot where I. C. had put the chair and the bowl with the hair dryer and toaster in it. The spot was vacant. I. C. went to the bathroom to see if the hair dryer was there.

"It's here!" he screamed from the bathroom. "Luca, go look inside the cabinet where you got the bowl and check the kitchen counter for the toaster." Luca ran to the cabinet and then to the kitchen.

"They're both here. And the chair is where it was."

"How do you feel?" I. C. asked Laura.

"I feel strange, but I believe you. I believe you. I'm just surprised that I don't remember anything. And what do you mean she was old and young at the same time?"

"She appeared as a pretty lady, young with long black hair and blue eyes. Then she changed to the way we always see her, old with the gray thing, the bun," Luca explained.

"She is protecting you from that creature," I. C. added.

"It wasn't a dream, Laura," Luca said. "It really happened right here. You fell and hit your head and became unconscious, and… who is…or what is…that horrible-looking monster? Lily called him Nogar or something like that."

"She saved me from him again?" Laura trembled as she remembered what appeared to have been her dream. "Why is he after me?" Laura cried as the boys tried to console her.

Laura, Luca, and I. C. sat on the sofa—each engrossed in private thoughts, each trying to figure out what had just happened.

Mrs. Williams broke the silence as she entered. She said that it had stopped raining as she came in with shopping bags.

"We'd better go," Laura spoke softly to Luca. On their way home, Luca tried to change Laura's mood by talking about I. C.'s new interests.

"He wants to change his nerdy image. He's into bodybuilding, he's listening to heavy metal, and who knows what else he's planning." Luca waited for Laura to respond but heard nothing. He kept on talking about I. C., but Laura was preoccupied. She thought about what had been a dream to her and was deathly afraid of what to expect next. She was comforted knowing that Lily had come to her rescue, but she questioned why Lily had entered her life, why she needed protection, and why that creature was after her. Not having any answers frightened her.

After a short period of silence, Luca asked, "What's with Lily? I think we almost lost her. Do you think she *can* die? And...and we almost lost you too."

"I don't know," Laura answered. "I know just as much as you do. I don't know what to say." She looked at Luca and forced a smile. They each went home on their separate ways.

Chapter 12

"I just ordered the pizza," Mrs. Stephens told Laura as she walked through the door. "Please set the table. It'll be here in twenty minutes. Where's Jeff?"

"Coming," Jeff answered.

When the pizza arrived, Mrs. Stephens and her two children sat at their places at the dining table. She tore off one regular slice for Laura, one slice with extra cheese for Jeff, and one slice of the same for herself. Laura stared at Jeff and her mother, not knowing what to expect.

"The pizza is good, as usual," Mrs. Stephens said.

"Yeah, good as usual," echoed Jeff.

"So-o-o how was your day, Jeff?" Mrs. Stephens asked as she reached for her wineglass.

"Okay except for the weather," Jeff remarked.

"And yours, Laura?"

"Okay. It was okay," Laura muttered. As she recalled the events, she felt chilled.

"How many books did I. C. read?" Mrs. Stephens asked.

"Eight," Laura remarked.

"Wow," Jeff laughed. "He really is a nerd." Jeff was nervous and was at a loss as what to say that would add something meaningful to the conversation. He was not happy with what had just come out of his mouth.

"I. C. is smart, and he really is *I* for intellectual and *C* for curious. That's why he got that name," Laura defended her friend. *If you only knew what he did today,* Laura thought. She wanted to tell them about Lily and about the creature that was after her, but how? They would think that she'd gone mad. She had difficulty believing it herself.

They continued to eat in silence until Laura covered her eyes and began to cry. Jeff, too, became teary-eyed. Mrs. Stephens stared at Andy's empty seat and recalled one of the many times Andy had eaten pizza with them.

"Remember when Andy tried to tear off a slice from the pie and threw the whole thing on the floor?" Mrs. Stephens asked out loud.

"Yeah," Jeff chuckled. "And then he wanted to feed it to the goldfish."

"We'll always have the memories, won't we?" Mrs. Stephens asked her children. Jeff and his mother continued to share old memories of Andy as Laura held back her tears and stared at her pizza in silence. Laura desperately wanted to believe that her mom had not lost hope that Andy would be found. Mrs. Stephens went over to her children and gave each a hug. Jeff couldn't hold back his tears as Mrs. Stephens consoled both of them. She, too, openly displayed her grief and wept.

"I miss him, Mom," Jeff finally spoke.

"Me too," Laura responded.

"We will always love him and cherish the memories. And we have lots of pictures that go with the memories." Mrs. Stephens tried very hard to be the strong one.

Laura asked if she could be excused from the table.

"Sure," their mom answered reluctantly. "I'll clean up."

Laura went to her room without finishing her slice of pizza. She normally would have asked for another. Jeff began to clear the table and told his mother that Laura had hardly eaten. Mrs. Stephens stared at Laura's plate, but she said nothing. It had been her first attempt at trying to get the family back to its normal Friday night routine. She wiped the table and went to the living room with Jeff.

Elaine Stephens hugged her sixteen-year-old son and sighed out loud. *When will the pain go away?*

Laura fell asleep almost instantly that night, but Lily gently interrupted the start of her first dream. "Lily? You're here…You're here?"

"Are you ready to go to a special place?" Laura's eyes widened, and she nodded. Lily put her hand on Laura's shoulder, and they instantly found themselves in new surroundings.

"Where are we?"

"This is my home," Lily answered. "We're in my real home, in a place that you won't find on a map. It's in another dimension."

"This is your bubble?"

"Yes, this is my ccass'a. If you look around, you'll see other bubbles. They are traveling too, like us." Laura looked around and saw all different sizes of traveling homes. Some of them were very colorful and changed their appearance every few seconds. One was green at first and then changed to purple and then orange. The cotton candy clouds that Laura had seen twice before reflected the colorful pattern. A parade of multicolored bubbles floated in the air.

Lily's ccass'a was much bigger than the one Laura had been on the two previous occasions when Lily had transported her there. Her furniture looked very old, like the kind Laura had seen at her grandmother's house. Each piece had a nondescript shape.

"What color is your bubble, Lily?"

"Think of three colors, Laura." Lily waved her hand, and the light inside the bubble turned a pale blue then a pale red and then a pale yellow. As the colors of the bubble changed, so did the color of the furniture. A vibrant blue, red, and yellow were seen on the outside by the other travelers.

"That is so cool, Lily. Look at that one. It doesn't have colors like the others. It has a painting. That's the…the…"

"Yes, that's the *Mona Lisa*," Lily finished Laura's sentence and gave a hearty laugh. Laura pointed out the bubbles that seemed peculiar and fun to look at. One had black-and-white stripes, another had purple-and-white polka dots, and some had pictures of animals. She saw a green swan, a yellow dolphin, and a purple giraffe.

"Those are the show-offs, the vanity homes." Lily gave a hearty laugh.

One bubble that had an arrangement of white calla lilies whooshed by them. Lily remarked that that ccass'a needed to slow down. Laura marveled at the sights from Lily's bubble and felt peaceful. She felt as if the events that had altered her life had never taken place. She was certain that she was in the middle of a vivid dream, but it felt so real. "I don't understand this, and I really don't believe... is this a dream?" she asked. Laura's doubts were interrupted by Lily's comforting voice.

"We're above my homeland, Mmajjia, where I was born. Look down, Laura." Laura looked down and saw miles of meadows and green fields. Waterfalls cascaded into oddly shaped lakes and river. Two lakes were shaped like the *W* and the *B* of the alphabet. There was a multitude of trees and plants that she knew did not exist on earth. There were no words that she knew of that could describe them. Among them stood huge *U*-shaped structures that Lily said were docking stations for the ccass'as. Some of them were empty; some had bubbles safely secured on them.

"We're going to travel faster now so that we can get to the Carousel." There was excitement in her voice.

"The Carousel? We're going on a merry-go-round?"

"It's more than that, Laura. You'll see."

She waved, expecting the bubble to move, but it did the opposite. It slowed down, and then it came to a full stop. Laura was about to ask Lily why they were going there, but she was preoccupied with the bubble's sudden stop. She waved her hand again and mouthed words unfamiliar to Laura, but the bubble did not budge.

"Something is wrong. We should be moving faster, and yet we slowed down."

"Are we in danger?" Laura sat down and looked at Lily, who was suddenly behind a control panel that popped out of a desk-like piece of furniture. Her hands pressed down on two silver levers and then pushed two red triangles. The bubble struggled to move and rocked back and forth like opposing teams in a tug-of-war competition. After several unsuccessful tugs, a thunderous thud made Laura scream. She covered her ears and screamed again. The face of the hideous creature that tried to kidnap her surrounded the bubble.

"He can't hurt you in here, Laura. You're safe in my ccass'a. He's trying to scare you and detain us from going to the Carousel. I have to free the bubble from his grasp."

"How? Look! We're surrounded," Laura hollered. The pale blue, red, and yellow colors inside the bubble turned gray; it was getting darker by the minute.

"They know you are here, Laura. Those are Nnogarth's soldiers in the black bubbles. They want to stop us from going to the Carousel. Hopefully it's his last attempt…Don't be alarmed. My ccass'a has more power than they think." Lily waved her hand over the control panel three times. Each time, different buttons and levers were pressed and pushed. After the third time, the bubble groaned, lurched forward, and stopped. Laura closed her eyes, expecting to find herself safely tucked in under the bedcovers in her room. When she did open her eyes, she was still in Lily's ccass'a; the bubble would not budge. Lily waved her hand once more, but this time all the buttons and levers lit up like hundreds of fireflies on a summer night. The bubble gave a roar and submitted to her will. It shot straight up into the air, turned, and then followed the route to their destination.

"We're safe now, Laura. We're safe."

The bubble docked on a *U*-shaped structure that was similar to the ones she had seen while traveling above Lily's homeland. And in what seemed to be just a breath away, before them were gardens filled with flowers of assorted sizes, shapes, and colors. The sun's rays enhanced the colors of each petal as it shimmered on them. She had never seen such a magnificent sight.

In the middle of the gardens, there was a Carousel of flowers, not horses, moving up and down and around in a circle. Each flower had a curved stem and two petals that curved under into repetitive circles. Laura watched the flowers as they moved gently back and forth and then up and down in rhythm. Melodious tunes met Laura as she walked with Lily toward the Carousel. Each flower danced to its own melody, and yet all the melodies synthesized into one tune. As the flowers continued to move on the Carousel, a shower of blue, yellow, purple, and green star-shaped flowers slowly fell on them. Flowers of colors and shapes that Laura could never have imagined continued to fall.

"This is the place of the Enchanted Carousel." Lily guided Laura to the Carousel and instructed her to mount an empty flower. The flower stopped dancing to receive her. Lily called out, "IT'S TIME. IT'S TIME," and the flower continued its dance. Laura's spirits instantly changed. And for the first time in a long while, Laura laughed and laughed with great joy; she was experiencing the true happiness that was ever felt by a child who had ever ridden the Enchanted Carousel. As Lily watched Laura, she began to transform. When the transformation was complete, she turned into a young woman; the gray bun and the wrinkles were gone.

Laura witnessed the change and called to her, "Lily...Lily, what happened to you?" And then she asked, "What is happening to me? I feel different, like I'm waking up or something. What's happening, Lily? What's happening to *me*?" And again, she asked, "How did you change yourself?"

"Ride the Carousel, Laura. Ride the Carousel." After Lily spoke the phrase for the third time, Laura's flower stopped. Laura waited for Lily to explain, but she didn't. Lily stepped away. Suddenly, she saw an image of her father before her. "Dad? Dad...Dad! You're here too? But you're..." Laura couldn't finish verbalizing her thoughts.

"I want you to speak to your father so that you can learn the truth. The joy you will feel now will always be with you. Your father is not here, Laura. Just his image. As you ride the Carousel, the pain that you have carried with you will vanish. But most of all, you will take part in the dance as you embrace the eternal energy of light and love."

Laura rode the Carousel and watched images of the accident without sorrow. Laura's father spoke to her.

"You see, Laura, after the accident, I began to drink. I didn't want to think about losing Andy. The drinking made me forget the accident."

"But, Dad, I saw the accident. The other driver hit you."

"I know, but I kept thinking that I could have done more. I don't know. Maybe I should have been more alert, or maybe I should have done something different, tried to fight, but I was paralyzed. I couldn't move. The drinking made me feel numb. Mom knew why I drank and that I had to leave to get help. I was not the person I used to be. As soon as the treatment is over, I'll come home. Mom tried to explain all this to you, but you didn't believe her."

"The kids in school said that you went to jail because you were drunk and caused the accident. I figured Mom was hiding the truth from me and that you really were in jail. And I'm the one who sent you out to get me the bobby pins. If I hadn't been so selfish, the accident never would've happened. It's my fault."

"It's no one's fault, honey. You have to believe that. It was meant to happen. You were meant to meet Lily. I was happy to get the bobby pins for your special night. I was proud of you then, as I am now. I love you, Laura. I'll be home soon." The Carousel stopped. The images faded, and Lily appeared again. She motioned Laura to walk with her to a dome-shaped gazebo near the Carousel.

"Laura," Lily began, "how do you feel?"

"I feel…I feel…happy. Yes, I feel happy. It's like I love everything and everybody and everything and everybody loves me. I've never felt like this. This place is amazing. It must be a dream and… and you brought me here. Why? Why me?"

"Nnogarth wants to destroy *you*. He tried to abduct you that day when you collapsed in the street, when you went to the city, when you went to Charles Street, and when you were unconscious at I. C.'s house. He usually preys on children who are weak in body and spirit. Your pain, your guilt, and most of all, your grief make you an easy target for him. This is why I have protected you and brought you here."

"It can't hurt me anymore?" Laura asked.

"You will become whole today, Laura, but still…that's…"

"Lily, what are you saying?" Laura screeched. "But what?"

"It's time you know the truth. Nnogarth can still make attempts to kidnap you until you turn thirteen years old."

"But that's not until April, April 11."

"I know, Laura, but he's especially after *you* for another reason. And for *that* reason, he will be always after you."

Laura was stunned and could barely make sense of what Lily had just said. Lily's words kept repeating in her mind.

"Why me? Why me?" Laura was finally able to verbalize her thoughts.

"That will become clear after you complete your ride on the Enchanted Carousel. You will become whole today. You will be the Laura that everyone has missed."

Lily's words soothed Laura, and some of her fears vanished. They walked back to the Carousel. Lily sat on one of the regal flowers with purple petals. It was the largest one there, and it shone the brightest. The Carousel began to move almost in slow motion. As it moved, Lily's appearance changed from young Lily to old Lily, old, young, old, young. The flashes stimulated Laura's memory. She instantly recalled what Luca and I. C. described to her that day at I. C.'s house. *This is what they meant,* she thought. Red, blue, and yellow lights played on Lily's changing body. She appeared to be communicating with spiraling lights. The multicolored spirals slowly moved away from Lily and hovered above her. Lily motioned for Laura to join her. The Carousel stopped momentarily to allow Laura to sit on the flower close to Lily. She held on to the petals not knowing what to expect. The spiraling lights came down on Lily and Laura and suspended them in midair for an instant. They were then returned to their flowers and began to move. Suddenly, the lights lifted the two passengers and their flowers into the air above the Carousel.

"Where are we going?"

"We're going to the other side." Lily and Laura landed on the far side of the Enchanted Carousel. This area was most extraordinary. There were fixtures as tall as houses shaped like pyramids made of mirrors. The flowers, trees, and foliage were all made of mirrors reflecting their images as well as the others. Laura saw her reflection in many peculiar shapes, sizes, and forms. One was so bizarre, it reminded her of a Picasso painting the art teacher had shown to her class last semester. That particular painting was composed solely of various geometric triangles, rectangles, and squares. One of the squares was a woman's face. Laura's reflection was just like the woman in the painting. Lily led Laura into one of the fixtures that had glass diamond-shaped panels from floor to ceiling. At first, she thought they were mirrors, but she realized that they weren't, for she did not see her reflection. The ceiling and the floor were made of what seemed to be crystal tiles in red, blue, and yellow, the colors of Lily's ccass'a.

They sat on cushions and faced one of the glass panels.

"Laura, what I'm about to show you is happening in Mmajjia, my home." As Lily spoke, images flashed on the panels. "Nnogarth is building up his manpower, his army, to fight for him and with him. You see, Laura, my beloved country, Mmajjia, is in the midst of a war. Nnogarth and his army have committed unspeakable crimes and want to take over the country and control my people. There are many brave Mmajjians who are fighting him, and they are gaining some ground." Lily hesitated. "You see, Laura, Nnogarth kidnaps children from your world and Mmajjia to make them part of his army. We must stay ahead of him if we are to succeed."

"He has an army of children?"

"No. When the children are taken to his camp, his scientists turn them. They transform them into soldiers with no memory of who they were or where they came from. They become robotic soldiers." Lily sighed. The images stopped. Lily looked out into the distance. "The children cease to exist when their new forms take over. They lose their youth, their childhood—they lose everything. The population of children in that part of Mmajjia has been drastically reduced because he abducted so many of them. Not only are the Mmajjians fighting the tyrant but they are also fighting to protect their future, their children. The children who remain are hidden and protected until they are thirteen years old. They can't be harmed after that magical day of their thirteenth birthday. That's something we still don't understand. Nnogarth tried to take you and abducted hundreds of other children. I was able to save you, but we lost many to him. There are more like me, Laura. We want to destroy Nnogarth and his army and save what's left of the Mmajjian youth. We need more Mmajjian warriors to prevent his army from growing and gaining power."

"Is Andy one of his soldiers?" Laura's voiced cracked as she spoke in anticipation of Lily's answer.

"No, he's in a holding camp for now. He will be transported to his camp of soldiers and turned soon, but I don't know when. We must get that schedule."

"Why, Lily? Why my brother? Why me?" Laura screamed.

"Andy was kidnapped because *you* are his target. Kidnapping him, it made you weak and made you grieve. You were an easy target for him." Lily hesitated. "And you should know that you are not like the other children."

"What do you mean?"

"You have been chosen to be a Mmajjian warrior one day. You will be able to save children as I have saved you and the others from Nnogarth's grasp." Laura was aghast with excitement. Her mind spun with questions.

"When will I become a warrior? Can we get to the camp? What about Andy...can we save him? What about Andy?" she repeated. "How can I help? Please, Lily, I want my brother back. Please, Lily," Laura cried out. Tears filled her eyes.

"Please understand, Laura. I've tried to get the schedule and have not been successful—yet. Also, the camp is surrounded with an invisible shield, a force field that my Mmajjian warriors and I have not been able to break down to infiltrate it. However, whenever Nnogarth deems it's the right time to transport the children, the shield opens to allow the transportation of the children. The opening is very small, just big enough for one of their military bubble to enter the camp. The entrance is heavily guarded on the ground and in the air. There are other factors that we need to consider before we attempt a rescue—the location of the camp, the time, and what type of bubble they use for transportation. We've tried to rescue Mmajjian children and children from your dimension, and sadly, more often than not, we failed. We either had the wrong location, the wrong time, the wrong type of transportation bubble, etcetera."

"You have to keep trying. You can't just give up." Laura's pleas continued.

"We haven't given up. We are working on it and are getting closer to getting all the information needed to get all the children out before they are turned. We haven't given up," Lily reiterated.

"I want to go there, Lily. I want to help you save my brother."

"That's out of the question, Laura. It will put you in harm's way. Nnorgarth is still after you. Remember, Andy was taken from you on purpose—to make you suffer and weak and…and vulnerable, an easy target. Do you see? And he knows you are *special.* You will always be a target. I can't risk it."

"When will I become a warrior…like you, Lily? When will that happen so I can help you rescue Andy? Please, Lily. I've got to know," Laura pleaded.

"You have to be at least thirteen years old, and even then, you'll be a young warrior, not strong enough to do battle with that evil creature. Your birthday is in April, Laura. We can't wait till then to rescue Andy. It will be too late. We have to rescue him while he's in the holding area."

"Make me a warrior now," Laura continued to plead with Lily. "Make me thirteen years old now."

"Hmm…I don't know how I can do that, how to cheat time, so to speak." Lily paused and looked away from Laura. "I would also have to find out if that's even possible." Lily did not sound very confident. Laura was very disappointed and disheartened to hear the uncertainty in Lily's voice. She thought there was nothing beyond Lily's power that couldn't be achieved.

Can it be done? Lily thought to herself.

"When will you know? When?" Laura pursued the answers.

"When its time. It's all in the timing," Lily replied. Lily's reply gave Laura hope and a sense of purpose now.

Laura glanced at the shiny fixtures, and both went back to the flowers that brought them there. The flowers landed on the Carousel and placed themselves on the spots that they had vacated. Laura looked at the majestic Carousel and wondered how long she'd have to wait.

"Goodbye, Laura. You'll find yourself in your room safely tucked in under your bedcovers." Lily smiled at her. "I'll see you next when it's time."

Chapter 13

The following day, Laura was called to the phone by her brother. He told her that their dad was on the phone.

"Hi, Dad...you are?...When? I can't wait... Now let's see what the kids in school will say. What? Yeah... Yes, I promise. Bye." Laura placed the receiver on the kitchen counter. Jeff called his mom so that she could continue her conversation with his dad.

"What did you promise Dad?" Jeff turned to Laura.

"That I'm going back to ballet school. Mom probably told him that I stopped taking ballet lessons," Laura quickly answered.

"You're really gonna take lessons again? I never thought you'd go back. Did Mom talk you into it? Did she raise your allowance or something?"

"No, but she told me she might get me a new cell phone if I promise not to go over the minutes and...to be careful not to lose it." Laura smiled.

Jeff hadn't seen such a big smile on his sister's face for a long time.

"Cool. Way to go."

Laura turned around and went up the stairs. Halfway up, she glanced back at her brother, who looked very puzzled. Laura tiptoed to her mother's room and waited outside the door. She listened for sounds but was relieved when she heard nothing unusual. She peeked at her wristwatch. It was only 8:20. Mom wouldn't be asleep yet. She softly knocked and then walked in. "Mom?"

"I'm running a bath, Laura. Anything wrong?" Mrs. Stephen's voice emanated from the master bathroom.

"No, nothing, Mom. I...I just wanted to see what you were doing. I just got off the phone with Dad. I told him that I'm going back to ballet school."

"I know. He just told me." Mrs. Stephens gave her a big smile and hugged her.

"I'm going to finish my homework and go to bed."

"Good night." Mrs. Stephens was pleasantly surprised. *This is a good sign. I hope she doesn't change her mind.*

Mrs. Stephen's mood turned somber as she thought of Andy. Her faith that Andy would be found had waned. Although she tried very hard not to show it, her heart ached for her son. She felt emptiness beyond description, bottomless.

Laura sat at her desk and stared at the porcelain blue-and-white ballet slippers. She went to her closet and searched for her pink ballet slippers, the pair she was to wear on opening night. They were wrapped in white tissue paper inside the white shoebox. She put them on and looked at her reflection in the mirror. She liked what she saw.

The following Saturday, Laura's mother dropped her off at the dance studio. Her tights, ballet shoes, and pink-and-white towel (the pink in the towel matched her slippers) were packed neatly in her sports bag. Her hair was pulled back and formed a bun slightly above the nape of her neck. Her mom drove away slowly and waved to her as her eyes searched for her reflection in the mirror. She waited until Laura entered the dance studio. She expected Laura to dash out at any moment, but Laura waved back and slowly walked to the lobby. Her preoccupation about remembering the various positions and the French terminology was interrupted by a familiar voice.

Laura heard the voice say, "Don't tell me you're back!" She turned around, and there in front of her was Jill.

"That's right. I'm back," Laura answered confidently.

"You missed so many lessons. Why bother?" Jill's tone annoyed Laura.

"Why do you care?" Laura continued to walk and was about to open the door to the studio.

"Who wants the daughter of a man…a man who's in jail taking lessons in this studio? I don't. And I bet no one else does either."

"My father is not in jail, so stop talking about him. And you should apologize for what you've been saying all this time." Laura stared at Jill without flinching.

"Everybody knows your father is in jail," Jill retaliated.

"Well, everybody is wrong. And everybody will know the truth. So let's begin with you. Apologize." Laura threw her sports bag on the ground and put both hands on her waist and spread her feet apart. "I'm waiting, Jill. APOLOGIZE!"

"So where was he? If he wasn't in jail, where did he go after the accident?"

"He went out of town on a business trip. That's where he went." Laura didn't feel proud about what she had just said, but it was too late to take back her lie.

"All this time, he's been on a business trip?" Jill laughed. Her screeching sounds wouldn't stop. She covered her mouth when she noticed Laura's eyes squinting and her lips protruding. She finally stopped laughing, but when her eyes met Laura's, she burst out laughing again. Laura wanted her hand to land across Jill's mouth so she would definitely stop cackling and concentrate on her painful lips. She imagined her hand sweeping across her lips several times until she begged Laura to stop and apologized. Her vision of Jill's face suddenly changed. Her anger began to subside despite her desire to silence Jill and finally have her revenge. She felt as if she were taking a ride on the Enchanted Carousel. She felt the wind on her face and heard the familiar melody; she became part of the rhythm, the colors, and its energy. Knowing the truth and becoming whole changed her and her desire to have revenge. Knowing that she would become a Mmajjian warrior and see Andy again made her fearless of the truth.

"My father is at a treatment center. He's getting cured…He started to…" Laura lowered her voice. "He started to drink after the accident. He blamed himself for it, but it wasn't his fault. Even the police told him that the other guy caused the accident, but my father felt responsible for Andy's disappearance. The drinking made him forget. That's why he drank. Now he's not drinking anymore, and he doesn't have to. He knows that he tried to avoid the accident. He believes that now and...and he'll be home soon. Now that's the truth! Why don't you spread that around?" Laura's trancelike state came to an end, slowly and gently. She picked up her sports bag and went inside the studio. She was amazed by her long unrehearsed response; the words had flowed one after the other. The knowledge of the Carousel and Lily surfaced in Laura's mind. She remembered Lily's words, and she saw the Carousel. She didn't want to visualize the Carousel; it just happened...or...did she make it happen? She wasn't sure.

Jill remained still outside the studio with her mouth slightly open as if she were about to catch a fly or two. She wondered why Laura had not hit her.

Chapter 14

Laura's father came home from the rehabilitation center, and as I. C. had predicted, the rumors about him and the accident stopped and were replaced by some other gossip that grabbed everyone's attention. And if Laura suspected that a seventh- or eighth-grader whispered something about her, she ignored it and didn't feel compelled to act on it. "And that," she said, "felt good." She felt good about many things; her family was healing. Laura was so delighted that her father was home that she suggested to her mom that they have a get-together for him. At first, Mrs. Stephens didn't agree to it, but Laura's enthusiasm changed her mind. She hadn't seen that spark of excitement in her daughter's eyes for such a long time she just couldn't ignore it. She agreed and made the phone calls.

The day finally came, and Mr. Stephens was surrounded by warmth and love of his close friends and family. Laura watched him with pleasure and joy as he greeted her friends and their parents. It warmed her heart to see her mom and dad mingle with their friends as laughter filled the rooms that had seen so much sorrow and tears. Her eyes welled up, and she wished that Andy was there. She closed her eyes, and in the darkness, she saw young Lily, with long black hair and blue eyes. She winked at Laura and gave her a big smile. She didn't know what to make of it, but just seeing Lily, even for just an instant, took away her sadness. It could only mean one thing; the time was approaching to save Andy. As she opened her eyes, she saw her mom engrossed in conversation. She was telling her friends how she impulsively had decided to go to the hair salon to get a new hairdo. Her chestnut shoulder-length hair was cut evenly below the chin and now glistened with auburn highlights. The top was combed over to the right side and gently rested on her right eyebrow. She remarked that she hadn't as yet become used to the new hairdo but was beginning to like it. Mr. Williams, I. C.'s father, remarked that she had a strong resemblance to an actress, the star of many motion pictures, whose name presently escaped him. As names were blurted out to identify the actress, Mr. Williams shook his head. He was at a loss; he simply couldn't remember her name. He looked to his son for help, but I. C. shrugged his shoulders and mouthed "I don't know" and went into the kitchen for a second helping of dessert.

"I. C. certainly is tall for his age," remarked Mrs. Stephens.

"Tall and lanky," added Mr. Williams. "A friend of mine once told me that my son is probably the black version of Abraham Lincoln as a youngster. My son loved the comment. In fact, he remarked that their intelligence should have been compared as well as their appearance."

"That certainly sounds like your son!" Mrs. Stephens said, smiling.

That night, Laura felt strange, unsettled. She couldn't fall asleep. She turned from side to side and kept trying, but something was just not right; she felt flushed. She sat up and saw Lily smiling at her.

"Lily?" She smiled back.

"We have to get back to the Enchanted Carousel," Lily quickly answered. Before Laura was able to respond, they were in Lily's ccass'a.

"It's time, Laura." Laura was all smiles to hear that familiar phrase. Laura noticed that Lily seemed unsettled too.

"What's wrong, Lily?"

Lily hesitated and then spoke as if she were out of breath, "We need to get to the Carousel as soon as possible. Nnogarth is coming for you. He found out about our plan and will do anything to stop us. We have to get to the Carousel tonight and make you a Mmajjian warrior."

"Tonight? You found a way? Are you able to do it?" Laura couldn't contain her excitement.

"I'll explain when we get there, Laura. Right now, we need to get you there." No sooner had Lily finished her sentence, they found themselves in her bubble. Suddenly, three of Nnogarth's dark, ominous bubbles appeared and surrounded them. Lily maneuvered her bubble and sped away, but they were in pursuit and were directly behind her again. Once again, Lily sped away from their grasp and managed to gain some ground.

"Look, Lily, there's more of them ahead of us," Laura cried out. "There's so many of them. We're surrounded. What are we going to do? I'm afraid."

"There are too many of them for me to fight off. I have to find a way to elude them and send for help." Lily pressed two blue levers up, down, and sideways as she spoke. "I know you're afraid, but have faith in me that we can do this. I'm going to change the shape of the ccass'a and make it smaller and thinner so it can squeeze through them. It can't remain in that state long, so we have to put it on maximum speed and make some headway before they are aware of our escape." No sooner had Lily stopped talking than Lily grabbed on to Laura's hand, and instantly the thin sphered ccass'a that now looked like a giant pancake took on the speed of light and sped away. The dark menacing bubbles were nowhere in sight, and the ccass'a returned to its original shape. Laura was stunned and remained motionless.

"I feel dizzy, Lily. I think I'm going to throw up," Laura mumbled. Lily quickly surrounded Laura's body in white light, and Laura felt relief. They continued to travel to their destination when suddenly the ccass'a came to a halt. The bubble became dark, as a black netted veil covered it. Lily pressed the three blue levers again three times to escape, but the ccass'a hardly moved. The hold of Nnogarth's bubbles was far too strong for Lily. Her bubble would not budge. Lily's bubble kept getting darker and darker inside and out.

"Lily, we need help. What are we going to do?"

"My warriors will come before our bubble heats up and disintegrates. We can't give up." Lily's voice was comforting, but Laura sensed fear in Lily's tone. The temperature kept rising. Laura felt sick and fainted. Lily enveloped her in the white light again. As soon as she regained consciousness, she cried out, "We're going to die, and...and...Andy will die too." Her sobs reverberated throughout the ccass'a.

"Not if I can help it. They're here, Laura." Lily's warriors, in their blue-and-white ccass'as, engaged in combat with the black and gray military bubbles that had their hold on them. As the battle ensued, Lily was able to free her bubble and sped away. She signaled the commander of her warriors to ward off Nnogarth's army of bubbles as long as possible. Lily sped away, but she knew that Nnogarth would not give up. His bubble pursued her, and as he gained speed and distance, Laura screamed. "Lily, he's getting closer and closer! Please do something!" she screamed louder. Lily did not respond. She stood still and posed with her arms outstretched in front of her as she faded in and out changing forms—young Lily, old Lily, young Lily, old Lily, following the same pattern that Laura had witnessed before—but this was different. Lily appeared as a child, a young adult, young Lily, old Lily, and kept changing forms simultaneously. Her arms seemed to be summoning someone or something. Just as Nnogarth's dark bubble was at arm's length and about to attack, the Enchanted Carousel appeared and enveloped Lily and Laura's bubble and swept them away. The Enchanted Carousel gently landed on the ground as the two passengers rode it.

"Lily, we're safe. We're safe," she repeated. "What's happening to me?"

"It's time, Laura. it's your time."

Laura's eyes filled with tears. She simultaneously felt strong feelings of empathy, compassion, joy, peace, and unconditional love for all creatures. She didn't think it possible that she was capable of experiencing such grandness. Her body felt warm sensations and cool sensations; every part of her body came alive and demanded her attention. She was immersed with feelings and sensations unbeknownst to her. Laura then elevated into the air and went into a metamorphosis. Lily gazed and smiled at Laura as an infant, as a child, as a teenager, and as a Mmajjian warrior. Lily then enveloped her in the white resplendent light, as she had done several times before, but this was extraordinarily different. Lily became part of the light, and she and Laura merged and became *one* with the Carousel. The newly formed entity gently spiraled into the air as vibrant colors zigzagged like lightning and danced around it. The glorious dance continued; the colors changed continuously and then settled into a multitude of shades of sparkling yellow and gold. Red, blue, and silver sparks flew into the air, accompanied by magnificent beams of light and then fireworks. Laura didn't just see the fireworks; she *became* the fireworks. She was the essence of the majestic lights. Her senses and her being were evolving, transforming. Slowly her body formed and emerged. Lily's eyes were fixed on her, and she smiled.

"It's done."

"Lily, you did it!" Laura exclaimed.

"No, the Enchanted Carousel answered our prayers. I don't have that ability. It's your destiny to be a warrior. I pleaded your case to hasten the process because we need to save *your* brother, Andy. As a Mmajjian warrior, you can be by my side. In your dimension, your world, you will celebrate your thirteenth birthday on April 11 as expected."

"Lily, the Carousel is gone," Laura gasped. "What happened?"

"The Carousel as you know it—its shape, the flowers, and so on—is an illusion."

"I see," Laura responded with a new robust voice, filled with confidence. "Was it a symbol?"

"Yes, a symbol for the force of eternal energy of light and love, E'ELL. It's the energy that is the unifying factor in the universe. It encompasses *all.*"

Laura suddenly became anxious and asked, "Can Nnogarth still hurt me?"

"Yes, in your world and in Mmajjia. He can and will always try to hurt you. You are a threat, just as I am. All warriors are. Kidnapping Andy was a means to get to you...Remember, he wanted you. He wants *you.*"

"Will he go after my friends, I. C. and Luca?"

"I don't think so—he might..." Lily hesitated. "Only if he thinks he can get to you through them. You are a threat to him. They aren't, but unfortunately, he's unpredictable," she continued.

"But...but I can protect them until they turn thirteen," Laura exclaimed.

"Yes," Lily interjected. "You'll be able to protect them until they both turn thirteen years old."

Laura sighed with relief knowing that she would be able to protect her two best friends.

"Our work here is done, Laura. There's more to be done to rescue Andy." Lily hesitated for a moment. A big smile framed her face; her eyes sparkled more than usual. "We have found the location of the camp."

Laura couldn't contain her excitement. She laughed so hard that her laughter turned to tears. "Thank you. Thank you," she repeated. She hugged Lily as tight as she could and couldn't pull herself away from the embrace. She was elated that she was going to see Andy again. "When, Lily? When?"

"That's our next challenge. I'll come for you, my young Mmajjian warrior, when all is in place and the time is right."

Chapter 15

L aura was back in her room, in her warm bed. A sea of images flashed in her mind as she reflected on her incredulous life-changing events. The urgency to save Andy increased with each thought and image. She wondered how soon it would be and how it would be accomplished. She felt the urge to scream and make an announcement to the whole town that the little boy, Andy, who had mysteriously disappeared was found. As her images faded, she, too, slowly faded and fell asleep.

The next morning, Laura wondered if her experiences with Lily and the Carousel had been a dream; she didn't feel different. Her thoughts shifted. If indeed it was her new reality, she wondered if she had the same powers as Lily. Did she have the capacity to heal, the strength and courage to battle Nnogarth and his soldiers, transport herself to Lily's ccass'a...or would she have her own bubble? What would it be like to be a Mmajjian warrior? It all seemed surreal... her thirst for the answers could not be quenched. She prayed that all would be revealed soon. She decided to check herself out in the mirror to see if she looked different; she instantly became mesmerized. Vibrant pictures of her, the accident, the Enchanted Carousel, and Nnogarth flashed by. Visions of Andy, explosions, Mmajjian warriors, and the darkness frightened her. She became overwhelmed with emotions and sensations that the visions triggered. Suddenly all went black.

What happened?

Laura opened her eyes and looked around but didn't recognize anything. Nothing was familiar. This was not her room. She was in a ccass'a, her ccass'a? She was disoriented and confused. She closed her eyes and took a deep breath. She silently pleaded for Lily to appear and clarify. Lily did appear.

"Lily, what just happened?"

"You got a glimpse of the past, the present, and a speck of the future. This is your first tiny step into becoming who you were born to be."

Laura's perplexity began to disappear. She then called out, "Lily, before I fainted, I saw us, Andy...and..." Laura hesitated. "So...we are going to do it? We're getting Andy out, and this nightmare will end?"

"Yes and no," Lily answered. "Yes, that's the plan. And no, the nightmare will not end until Nnogarth is destroyed or at least stopped from abducting more children. His army has to be dismantled and weakened."

"I have questions, Lily, about my powers and how to use them and...and what does it really mean to be a warrior...and...I'm new at this. I need your help."

"You will instinctively know what to do and how to use the gifts you have. I can only guide you to the best of my ability. You may have abilities that I don't have or am not familiar with. Earlier you saw images just by looking in the mirror—I've never experienced that. You will probably continue to surprise me as you learn more about them and yourself. You are unique, unlike the other warriors."

"How am I so different?"

Lily hesitated, and another big smile framed her face. Laura waited anxiously for Lily to complete her thought, but Lily was in a trance. Her eyes flickered as if she were in a REM state of sleep while awake.

"You'll know, my dear. You will know. I'm being summoned, Laura. I must leave. I must save a Mmajjian child from being abducted." Before Laura could ask more questions, Lily was gone.

The day at school was strange for Laura. Her mind kept wandering, yet she was able to focus. *How peculiar*, she thought. She instantly grasped new concepts in her classes, anticipated the questions, and knew the answers to the questions the teachers posed. It was as if she were the teacher and the student simultaneously in all her classes. *This is crazy awesome*, she thought. The thoughts of the twelve-year-old Mmajjian warrior became playful, as she imagined silly things that she might be able to do in the classroom and to her classmates and teachers, but she quickly dismissed them, as it occurred to her that she had a mission to fulfill and *that* was serious. Saving Andy and fighting Nnogarth were very serious. She missed her little brother and hoped that he was not suffering in the holding camp. No sooner had she thought of Andy that young Lily appeared to her.

"They are going to move Andy and some of the children from the holding camp. This is what we were waiting for. We must go." Instantly, Laura found herself in Lily's ccass'a. Laura was surprised to see young Lily, for she usually appeared to her as the old woman with the gray bun.

The ccass'a was surrounded with hundreds of Lily's armies of bubbles ready to follow her orders. As the bubbles traveled toward their destination, Laura became fearful that they would not succeed. She tried desperately to dispel thoughts of doubt and failure. She found it difficult to be optimistic about the mission. She knew what Nnogarth was capable of and how he had almost killed her had Lily not come to her rescue. It was different now. She was at Lily's side to fight their common enemy, this evil creature that preys on innocent children and turns them into robotic soldiers to fight for him and his maniacal cause. Her young mind drifted again.

"Can Nnogarth be killed?" Laura asked.

"Yes, if *he* has a soul." Lily sighed. "There is a story—probably just that, a story—that he was a child who had been turned several times and experimented on by an unidentified force of evil, the antithesis of the Enchanted Carousel and E'ELL, the eternal force of energy, light, and love. He lost most of what was human about him and became what he looks like today, the grotesque apparition that he projects. No one knows what he really looks like. As he became stronger, he was favored to become the leader of the regions that his armies occupied. After a region is taken over by his soldiers, the area is renamed Nnogarthian Territory 1, 2, and so on. He was given the name Nnogarth, which means powerful and dominant."

"If he has a soul, then we can destroy him," Laura firmly stated.

"If the story has any validity, that would be possible," Lily answered. "Let's focus at the mission at hand now." Lily became very focused and posed her plan. "The camp's shield cannot be penetrated. The only way we can get to Andy is to wait for it to open. It only stays open for ten minutes at most, and it is heavily guarded. The children to be transported are very close to the opening so that Nnogarth's soldiers can easily swoop them in their funnel-shaped ship like a tornado swoops up whatever is in its way. These children will then be turned into Nnogarth's soldiers in his army camp. We can't fail," Lily exclaimed. "We don't know when the shield is scheduled to open again." The images that Laura had seen in the mirror flashed by in her mind as Lily spoke.

Lily and her army of bubbles approached the camp. They left behind the puffy cotton candy-shaped white clouds as the sky became dark and dim. The dark sky soon lit up like lightning during a thunderstorm. Enemy soldiers shot at them with striped black-and-white arrow-shaped missiles that cloaked the target with a heavy net that propelled it out into space. Many of the bubbles were instantly hit and catapulted out of the battlefield and disintegrated. The Mmajjians courageously fought back with radiant blue missiles to clear a path for Lily's bubble to get to the opening. Nnogarth's soldiers, in gray metal suits and blank-and-white striped triangular helmets that exposed only their yellow oval-shaped eyes, robotically shot more missiles at them from the holding area on the ground. Laura was horrified with the thought that these soldiers were once children whom Nnogarth had abducted, indoctrinated, turned, and trained to be his soldiers. The troubling thought that these were once children kept repeating in her mind. As she saw some of them die at the hands of the Majjians, her heart felt heavy. Was Andy to be one of these soldiers…was this the fate that awaited her little brother? The possibility of that reality hit her hard.

As the battle raged all around Lily's fortified bubble, Lily waited for the opportune moment to transform her ccass'a into the size of a pancake, as she had done once before when Nnogarth's army was pursuing her. As her bubble sped to the opening, Nnogarth suddenly appeared and attacked. His two attempts failed, as Lily maneuvered the bubble side to side, in circles, and then zigzagged upward. She then disappeared and returned in top speed as she dodged the soldiers' missiles, but one of the arrow-shaped missiles scraped Lily's bubble on the side. Nnogarth roared in delight. Lily instantly withdrew to the side and sped away. She assessed the damage to be minimal and returned with more determination. Time was of the essence. She had to reach the opening and get to the children before they were swooped away. Several of the bubbles that were in front of her were hit. As they were flung into space, one of them hit Lily. Lily's bubble became entwined with it and almost was catapulted too. Lily struggled to free herself from the Mmajjian bubble, but she couldn't. She knew what had to be done.

"If I don't destroy that Mmajjian bubble, we..."

"You have to kill your warrior?" Laura cried out.

"No, just destroy the bubble so that we can be free from it and not be decimated and reduced to ashes along with it." Laura watched in awe as Lily transported the Mmajjian soldier into her bubble and watched the bubble disintegrate from a safe distance. She was ashamed that she had the ugly thought that Lily could possibly harm one of her Mmajjian soldiers or anyone for that matter.

"We don't have much time left. We have to head back toward the opening," Lily exclaimed. The Mmajjian soldier expressed to Lily that she would be more helpful if she were transported into another bubble and rejoin the troops. She instantly was, and Lily directed her bubble back to its destination, the aperture to the holding camp.

Lily's bubble metamorphosed into a large pancake, which Laura was now used to seeing, and sped away. In flight, she battled Nnogarth's bubbles and almost got hit again had she not used her evasive maneuvers. She was about to land her bubble and approach the camp when Nnogarth appeared again. He was stronger and bigger than their last encounter. He pulled her bubble toward him. Lily and Laura abandoned their bubble; they knew they had to face him. Laura shivered as they got closer to him amidst the battle that raged on the ground and in the air.

Don't be afraid, Laura. You have powers now. You are a Mmajjian warrior, Lily telepathically assured her. Lily instructed her to take all the warriors available and save the children. She was going to battle Nnogarth.

The Mmajjian warriors followed Laura to the opening of the camp to rescue the children and Andy. They fought the guards holding the children as they were about to be swooped up in their bubble and transported to the army camp. They were attacked with rocket-shaped projectiles that would instantly paralyze them, followed by death. Laura instinctively enveloped them in a brilliant white light, as Lily had done to her so many times. Unfortunately, she couldn't get to all of them in time, and many Mmajjian warriors perished. Laura fought bravely, but she knew that she couldn't continue to ward them off and go unscathed for too long. She had to get to the children; she had to rescue Andy. She was shocked to see dozens of children with Andy marching toward the bubble that was to transport them. She hardly recognized Andy but couldn't react. She didn't have the time to hug him or tell him how much she had missed him or that she was taking him home. She instantly enveloped him and as many children as she could with her brilliant light. Suddenly, Nnogarth appeared, and he, too, tried to stop her. He covered her and the children with the black veil that almost killed her the day on Charles Street with Luca. She was able to remove the black veil, but many of the children, including Andy, were suffocating as the veil covered their bodies. Again, Laura enveloped them in her resplendent white light and transported them into Lily's bubble. Nnogarth was swift and covered the bubble with the black translucent veil, preventing the bubble from taking off. Lily followed Nnogarth and hit him with a ball of light to stop him, but he was unrelenting. Again, she pounded him, harder this time, but Nnogarth was unstoppable. Meanwhile, Laura and the children were helpless, as the bubble became hot and dark inside. The two continued to battle as Laura watched and prayed that Lily and her warriors would prevail and defeat Nnogarth so they could be freed. She stared at the children and Andy, who were in a catatonic state, unaware of their fate. Laura tried to revive them but was unsuccessful. She wanted to reach out to her brother, but he, like the others, was unresponsive, lifeless. She didn't know how much time she had and called for Lily to save them. Lily heard her cries as she fought valiantly with Nnogarth. Lily metamorphosed into young Lily, old Lily, young Lily, and old Lily. As she transformed, she hit Nnogarth again, to no avail. She raised her arms into the air and summoned for help. Instantly, the Carousel appeared. Nnogarth's creepy thunderous roar could be heard for miles on end. His soldiers stood still like statues as they witnessed Lily, the Carousel, and E'ELL merge into one. This brilliant sight allowed the Mmajjians warriors to return to their bubbles and took off. Lily simultaneously repaired and transported her bubble to the land of the Enchanted Carousel. Nnogarth's howls and roars of defeat were heard from a distance as they continued on their way.

Chapter 16

The bubble landed at the Enchanted Land of the Carousel. Lily and her new warrior escorted the children to the Carousel and placed each one on a flower. As they rode it, Lily and Laura transformed into young Lily, old Lily, Laura as an infant, Laura as a teenager; the transformations continued on and on. Each form shined like a bright star in the dark sky.

Each Mmajjian child and Andy was placed on a flower of the Carousel. Lily and her young warrior placed their hands on the curved petals as it gently rocked back and forth and up and down in rhythm. They were showered with star-shaped flowers as the Carousel danced to the rhythm and melodious harmony of the universe. Lily and Laura transformed to their various young and old appearances and were delighted to see that the children were responding one by one. They were coming out of their stupor. The boys smiled, and their blank looks disappeared, and some of the girls reached for the flowers and reveled at the sight.

"RIDE THE CAROUSEL," Lily and Laura exclaimed in unison. And that they did! The music of laughter resounded throughout the land.

"Laura, Laura," Andy called out, "look at these funny flowers." Laura rejoiced upon hearing Andy's voice. She joined Andy and stood by him as they both rode the majestic Carousel. She held him close to her, afraid to let go of him. *I've missed you so much*, she thought. She felt guilty for having put him in harm's way. She imagined how her mom and dad would react and feel to have their son returned to them. The Carousel slowly stopped. Andy broke his sister's embrace, unaware of the circumstances that had brought him there.

"I like this merry-go-round. Can we stay on it for another ride?" Andy's enthusiasm and laughter warmed her heart. "Can we go on more rides?" Andy called out.

Laura glanced at Lily for answers. Lily communicated to her to take the children to the other side where she herself had been not too long ago. Laura, Andy, and the healed children dismounted their flowers and began walking.

"Andy, this is my friend, Lily. Want to say hello?" Andy murmured a hello and held on to Laura's hand.

They gingerly walked on the path familiar to Laura. When they turned to reach the far side of the Carousel, however, the area was now an amusement park. Gone were the pyramid-shaped fixtures and the mirrored flowers and foliage that reflected one another. Lily winked at Laura as Andy and the children ran to go on the rides. They rode the flying coaster, crazy dinosaur, bumper cars, and other kiddie rides to their delight.

Lily and her young warrior sat on a bench and watched Andy as he rode the caterpillar ride that swayed from side to side and backward. He laughed with abandon and waved as he screamed with joy.

"What happens now, Lily? Will Nnogarth still be after him?"

"I'm afraid so. He's the link to you, but *you* will be able to protect him, and I will be by your side. There are many Mmajjian children to be saved and not enough warriors to help me. And what makes matters worse, the location of the holding camp and the transportation schedule change as well. I need more warriors." Lily's voice changed to one of desperation.

"Why not make Luca and I. C. warriors?" Laura asked with anticipation.

"That's not possible. All my warriors are Mmajjian."

"I don't understand. You made me a warrior, and I'm not from your dimension."

"You are an exception. You are unique, *special*. It was *your destiny* to be a warrior."

"Why me? What is *special* about me?"

"You will know when it's time." Laura was annoyed with Lily's answer. She was still not used to Lily putting off the answers to her questions.

"Let's get the children back to their families," Lily firmly stated.

Chapter 17

Laura yawned as she glanced at the clock. The digital clock showed 8:45. She heard voices and music coming from the kitchen. "I'm home. Oh my God, I'm home." She couldn't contain her excitement. "Is Andy here?" she spoke out loud. She put on her slippers and ran downstairs. She saw Andy across from the kitchen watching cartoons in the living room.

"Andy, Andy, *you're* home. You're home," she repeated. Her eyes couldn't believe the wondrous sight.

"Of course, he's home, Laura. Where else would he be on a Saturday morning?" Mrs. Stephens asked. "Come and have breakfast," she continued. "I made pancakes."

"Oh...um...I...I...I had a bad dream, a very bad dream," she called out.

"Well, that's all it was, a bad dream." She hugged Laura and again told her to eat her pancakes before they got cold. Laura didn't want to make a fuss and contained her excitement. She sat down and poured syrup on her pancakes and began to eat.

"I have to go to the office today and then host an open house. I'll be gone a few hours. Please watch Andy, okay?" Laura didn't answer. She had not processed what she had heard. "Laura, did you hear me? I asked you to watch Andy. Daddy and Jeff are out." Mrs. Stephens walked to the front door and waited for Laura to respond.

"Sure, Mom. No problem," Laura finally answered as her mom closed the door behind her. A cold winter's wind made an entrance into the kitchen, but Laura didn't react to it. She was overtaken with the joy of seeing Andy. She was baffled but pleasantly surprised that everything was back to *normal*. Looking after Andy took on a whole new meaning. She was now responsible for his safety, for his life. She was also responsible for Luca and I. C. until their thirteenth birthday. Suddenly her joy turned to fear. Tears rolled down her face with the realization that her loved ones were vulnerable to Nnogarth's attacks because they were linked to *her*. This weighed heavily on her; she questioned her abilities. She didn't feel like a warrior; she felt like a fragile young twelve-year-old. "Why me, why me?" she screeched. More tears ran down from her eyes to her lips. She stopped eating her favorite breakfast and got up. She paced around the kitchen and occasionally looked in on Andy, whose eyes were fixed on the TV.

Lily sensed her fear and appeared to her.

"I don't think I can do this, Lily. I'm responsible for Andy, my friends. I…I can't do this," she cried. "There's got to be someone else. Pick another person," Laura blurted out, forgetting the niceties of greeting her mentor and friend.

Lily sensed Laura's fear and rested her eyes on Laura for a short while. *Should I tell her?* she thought. *What should I do? I've always mentored Mmajjian warriors, but not someone like Laura, the* special *one.* Finally, she spoke, "*I* didn't choose you." Lily told her to sit down and relax. "You and E'ELL made that decision." Lily's soothing voice did not calm Laura.

"When…How…" Laura gasped. She covered her face with her hands in disbelief. Fear flooded her.

"In my homeland, Mmajjia, before you were born in this dimension, E'ELL conferred with you about this mission, and you accepted graciously without any reservations. You accepted your mission to save children from Nnogarth's wrath."

"You are saying that all Mmajjian warriors don't do this?"

"No, they volunteer their services when they are eighteen years of age." Lily couldn't tell her more than that at this time.

"So why did I do that…confer with E'ELL. Why?" Laura paced around the kitchen again, trying to process the information.

"That's between you and E'ELL."

"I don't get it. Lily...I...don't understand. I just don't get it," Laura cried out in despair.

Lily watched her intently and did something she had not done in a long time...she questioned the decisions she had made. Had she cheated time to make Laura a warrior too soon for the urgent need to save Andy? No. She and Laura had merged with E'ELL. She had received consent to do so. She was at a loss as to why Laura was regressing to prewarrior days. She had never experienced such behavior with other warriors. Was it to be expected with Laura? After all, *she was the exception*. And she was only a teenager. In desperation, Lily immersed Laura in various shades of green *healing* light with the white resplendent one. The brilliant shades of jade green and white light embraced Laura and elevated her in the air. She was on the Carousel; she was riding it, as she had done once before, and yet it was different. She relived the life-altering moments when she had felt alive and experienced unconditional love, when she became a warrior, when she courageously rescued Andy, and when she healed the Mmajjian warriors in battle. She felt empowered...she owned them.

When Laura touched the ground, she glowed for an instant and then acknowledged Lily.

"What's wrong, Lily? Why are you here?" she asked calmly. "Do we have to rescue a Mmajjian child?"

"No, I'm here because I sensed your fear. You questioned your abilities as a Mmajjian warrior." Lily broke the tension and added, "You needed to have your abilities tweaked." She chuckled and winked at Laura.

"*That's* funny," Laura giggled. "Did I lose them? What happened?"

Lily calmly recounted that she had regressed to prewarrior days and postwarrior concerns and fears.

"Yes, I kind of remember...the fear, my doubts...the fear," she repeated. Laura's green eyes assured Lily that she was fine now. "Those feelings are gone, Lily. I'm okay. Thank you, but," she added, "I still don't know why I was chosen."

"You will know when it's time."

Laura graciously accepted that answer. Laura, the Mmajjian warrior, had returned.

Lily and her young warrior embraced, and they both glowed.

"I hope *that* doesn't happen again…and I won't need another tune-up." They both laughed out loud.

"On a serious note, Lily, I'm a bit baffled. How will Andy's reappearance be explained?"

"*You* are a Mmajjian warrior…the *special* Mmajjian warrior. You will know, and your questions will be answered. I'm being summoned, Laura. I must go."

"Don't you need me?"

"No, Laura, I don't. I will summon you should I need your assistance."

Lily faded and disappeared.

Laura was suddenly flooded with information. She gained insight and answers to her questions. Her mom's remarks made sense now. It *all* made sense now. Her mom and probably everyone else didn't remember that Andy was kidnapped. *They don't remember anything at all.* Laura was grateful for that. They didn't remember the grief and the pain they went through. Luca and I. C. didn't remember their encounters with Lily and Nnogarth. Laura sighed with relief.

Laura knew that the war with Nnogarth was not over. Luca, I. C., and especially her brother were in danger until they each became a teenager. The sobering thought was that she would sense when they were in danger and had the ability to protect them, the same way Lily had saved her numerous times.

Why is becoming a teenager so crucial? She didn't want to bother Lily for that answer…she'd probably say that she'd get the answer *when it was time* anyway. And she left it at that.

Chapter 18

The school year continued, and the cold winter came to an end without any incidents or signs of Nnogarth. Laura, at times, had ominous feelings that he would attack without warning, but he didn't. She had not been summoned by Lily, nor had she had contact with her either.

The days grew longer. Signs of spring were evident. The trees gave birth to new leaves daily as tiny buds seemed to mature and blossom overnight. The clothing that the children wore also showed signs that the winter was over. The dark browns and gloomy blues were put to rest along with the boots and woolen socks.

Laura, I. C., and Luca walked home from school. Today, they decided to walk through the park instead of taking their usual route.

"Spring is my favorite time of the year. Everything around us changes. Everything seems to wake up," I. C. leisurely remarked. "I wonder what life would be without spring."

Each of them mused at the idea as I. C. began to verbalize his thoughts.

"We wouldn't have flowers, and the trees, of course, would be barren."

"No grass to sit on or play ball," Luca added.

"No birds or nests," Laura joined in.

"Oh no, we would have homeless birds!" exclaimed I. C. "And cement—cement everywhere. I would petition the government to build condos for the homeless birds," he added. I. C. laughed at himself as Luca laughed with him.

"There's Lily," I. C. announced as he pointed to a park bench ahead of them.

"Who?" asked Luca.

"Oh, we met her, I think. You probably...you probably don't remember her," I. C. answered.

"Oh, I remember," Luca said. "You helped her cross the street, and she asked us our names. Don't you remember, Laura?" Luca glanced at Laura, who seemed very puzzled.

Why is Lily here? Laura was astounded to see her and barely knew what to say. "Oh...I...I remember now. She said that she couldn't see very well, right?" Laura added to the conversation, still shocked at the sight of Lily.

"Yeah, I remember now. She told us her name...yeah. Yeah, she did," Luca continued.

"Yes! How can you forget? I remember the introductions and how I laughed at icy, my initials I. C., and then she said, 'I see.'" I. C. laughed as if he were hearing it for the first time.

Luca was puzzled; he didn't seem to remember the part that I. C. was referring to, but he laughed with him.

"Oh, there's Jill and Lisa," I. C. called out.

As Jill and Lisa passed by them, Jill looked back and broke a smile. Laura was relieved that the exchange between them was uneventful and continued to walk with the boys. As the boys chatted, Laura was engrossed in her private thoughts about Lily. She turned to wave to her but saw only her cane. She then appeared for an instant and vanished.

The threesome continued to walk, and after a brief silence, Laura called out, "Come on, guys. Let's go for ice cream before we go home."

"I'm taking off this jacket, and I'd be glad to accompany you," I. C. blurted out.

Luca eyed the cell phone in I. C.'s back pocket when he removed his jacket. "I'm taking this away and won't give it back to you until you talk normal!" Luca yelled as he raced away. I. C. ran after Luca, both forgetting about Lily, Jill, and Lisa.

Laura remained behind. She thought about Lily again. She then looked at the boys who were flinging their jackets in the air and smiled.

Lily visited Laura in her room that night.

"It was good to see you and your friends, Laura."

"I was surprised to see *you* today, and...and...you appeared to them. Why? Are they in danger? I haven't sensed Nnogarth's presence these past few months," Laura said.

"I'm concerned that Nnogarth is planning something big, hence his absence in this dimension."

"He's planning an attack?"

"Yes." Lily was solemn.

"Do you know who he'll attack or when this will happen?"

"I don't have the details—he's been hard to read. My visions are blurred. His monstrous ways have been more unpredictable than usual, and he's gained more power—I can feel it." Lily was unsettled. "He's still after you—*anyone* who's linked to you and hasn't had a thirteenth birthday."

"Yes, you mentioned that after we rescued Andy." Laura expected the bad news. "But we can protect them till then," she exclaimed with confidence.

"That's what troubles me—too many children are linked to you," Lily quickly answered.

"Why is that a problem?" Laura was perturbed. "Why, Lily?"

"I'm not confident that we will be able to protect them all. This time, he will attack to destroy." Laura was alarmed by Lily's tone. She sensed fear in her but couldn't pinpoint exactly what she was afraid of. "My Mmajjian warriors will not be able to assist us. They can only protect the children of Mmajjia. Only you and I are privileged to travel in both dimensions." Lily lowered her head and murmured, "I'm sorry."

The young warrior gazed at Lily. She felt let down, abandoned by her mentor and savior.

"I know that you will be very vigilant and you'll protect Andy and your friends. Laura, you know that *I will be by your side*. We will do whatever needs to be done to keep everyone safe."

Laura felt nauseous—fear overwhelmed her. *I wonder if I'll have my birthday party,* she thought. She was looking forward to celebrating her thirteenth birthday party in *her* world with *her* friends and family. Most importantly, she wondered if Luca and I. C. would be safe till *they* turned thirteen. Luca would turn thirteen in May, and I. C. in August. The responsibility weighed heavily on her shoulders—they were linked to her, and Nnogarth would stop at nothing to hurt her. He might even go after Lisa and Jill, whose birthdays are in September. *What about my other friends?* Laura became lost in her thoughts; her mind was reeling. Suddenly, for the first time, Laura sensed Lily's fear—*that* was too much for her to bear.

"I will be by your side, Laura. This is not the end," Lily assured her. With these consoling words, Lily left.

Lily's words, however, did not comfort Laura, the young Mmajjian warrior; they terrified her. Suddenly all went black.

About the Author

C arol Di Prima's career as an educator has spanned decades. She started her teaching career as an ESL (English as a second language) teacher for adults and then followed her calling and taught children in an elementary school where she taught grades K–5 in various positions and subjects, one of which was as the school librarian. Being the school library and media specialist intensified her passion for books and writing. It gave her great joy to see the look of wonder when her students read their favorite books.

Di Prima is a member of the American Library Association. She graduated from Lehman College and Syracuse University, with degrees in elementary education, intermedia, and SLMS (school library and media specialist). She lives in Westchester, New York, with her two cats, Sienna and Bella. *Lily…Laura* is her first published work.

CPSIA information can be obtained
at www.ICGtesting.com
Printed in the USA
BVHW081111180920
588316BV00002B/103

9 781662 411373